"That doesn't make any difference."

Roxanne's reply was quick; she refused to be browbeaten.

"No?" Guy uttered an expletive. "This morning you've dragged me out of bed, called me names, tried to batter me into submission on the TV series, and for what?" His nostrils dilated in disgust. "A sum of money which to you represents loose change."

"We're talking about thousands of pounds," she protested.

His eyes swept over her, assessing. "What would you spend it on? Perhaps some seductive low-cut outfits to entice rich husband Number Two?"

She balled her fists. "There won't be another husband, rich or otherwise," she declared. "I intend to go it alone."

Roxanne drew a shaky breath. It was so long since she'd been involved in any male-female byplay that she didn't know what to think—or do.

ELIZABETH OLDFIELD began writing professionally as a teenager after taking a mail-order writing course, of all things. She later married a mining engineer, gave birth to a daughter and a son and happily put her writing career on hold. Her husband's work took them to Singapore for five years, where Elizabeth found romance novels and became hooked on the genre. Now she's a full-time writer in Scotland and has the best of both worlds—a rich family life and a career that fits the needs of her husband and children.

Books by Elizabeth Oldfield

HARLEQUIN PRESENTS
1012—BEWARE OF MARRIED MEN
1030—TOUCH AND GO
1077—QUICKSANDS
1101—LIVING DANGEROUSLY
1132—CLOSE PROXIMITY
1212—SPARRING PARTNERS
1300—RENDEZVOUS IN RIO
1333—THE PRICE OF PASSION

ELIZABETH OLDFIELD

love gamble

Harlequin Books

TORONTO • NEW YORK • LONDON
AMSTERDAM • PARIS • SYDNEY • HAMBURG
STOCKHOLM • ATHENS • TOKYO • MILAN

Harlequin Presents first edition May 1991
ISBN 0-373-11365-X

Original hardcover edition published in 1990
by Mills & Boon Limited

LOVE GAMBLE

CHAPTER ONE

ROXANNE'S fingers tightened around the receiver. 'I'm going to kill Guy Slaney,' she decided.

'Could be the answer,' the voice at the other end of the telephone line agreed cheerfully. 'There'd be no resistance to a second showing of the series then.'

'And no one to swindle me out of my repeat fees. Who does the damn man think he is?' she protested. 'Four years ago he was happy enough to appear in *Assignment Paris*, yet now you say he's claiming it's bad for his image?'

'That's how the story goes. Of course, my information comes second-hand so I don't have his objections verbatim,' her friend pointed out. 'However, I do know he's blocked another run.'

'He has no right to do that!'

'Maybe not, but as the most talented young actor around he obviously wields the necessary clout. I dare say the people here are wary of upsetting someone who's destined to become a leading force, so it's a case of whatever Guy Slaney wants, Guy Slaney gets.'

'Success seems to be swelling his pretty little head,' Roxanne remarked pithily.

'I wouldn't call him pretty, or good-looking, come to that—but with those tiger eyes he certainly possesses a high tingle quotient,' Karen exalted, sounding like one of the magazines she so avidly read, but Roxanne had stopped listening.

'*I* shall upset him,' she announced. 'You say old High and Mighty lives within walking distance of me? I'll call round this morning.'

'Do you think you should?' her friend asked doubtfully.

'Why not?'

'But what'll you do?'

'Don't worry, I'll leave my machine-gun at home and sock him with some friendly persuasion instead,' Roxanne said, though the last thing she felt towards her erstwhile co-star was friendship. In the past they might have rubbed along fine, but by adopting such an autocratic attitude he had effectively turned himself into her enemy. 'He's not going to get away with this.'

'If you see him, don't mention my name,' Karen begged. 'What I've told you doesn't exactly rate as top secret, but if anyone discovered it was me who'd——'

'I'll be ultra-discreet. I shan't get you into trouble,' she promised, in firm reassurance.

'Thanks.'

'Thank you for alerting me to what's been going on behind my back.'

As a secretary employed by the television company which had produced the detective series, Karen was Roxanne's last tenuous link with the entertainment world. Although when they met they talked about a wide variety of subjects, from time to time her friend naturally referred to what was happening at work—and a month ago had passed on the news that *Assignment Paris* had been hauled from the archives. On hearing that the series was to be dusted off and scheduled for another showing, Roxanne had almost keeled over with shock. Repeats were a development she had never considered. Ever. Not that she was complaining—on the contrary, she had been delighted. However, minutes ago her delight had vaporised, to be replaced by fierce indignation. The actor's agent had, so Karen reported, advised the company that his client found the prospect of a rerun unacceptable, and now the spools were to be returned to the shelves.

'Friendly persuasion might work,' her friend mused. 'Anyone who watched the series could tell he was smitten with you.'

'Karen, he was playing a role. As a lusty French cop Guy was *supposed* to fancy me, that's all!'

'And you were the ice-cool private investigator from London who kept him at arm's length—mostly.' A sigh drifted from the telephone. 'The plots were far-fetched, but the casting was inspired. Full of chemistry.'

Roxanne shook a despairing head. Sensible in all other areas, when it came to show business Karen was as gullible as any starstruck schoolgirl. No matter how exaggerated or unlikely the publicity hype, she implicitly believed every word.

'Look, he was involved with Prue Graham at the time. As for me——' she frowned '—I had other things on my mind. I'll give you a ring and let you know what happens,' she went on quickly. 'Bye.'

An hour later, as she followed a route memorised from the street map, Roxanne rehearsed what she would say. She intended to be friendly, but firm. Guy Slaney might be merely indulging in the flexing of a vainglorious muscle or two, yet for her, and others, there was more at stake. Much more. The series had been deemed bad for his image—huh! She had not noticed any high-falutin tendencies in the days when she had known him, but now he deserved to be kicked for taking such a lordly view of himself and his career. Kicked, severely reprimanded, and brought down a considerable number of pegs—to ground level, where everyone else resided.

Roxanne curbed her irritation. Losing her temper would get her nowhere. Instead, she must summon up that calm and composed demeanour and act as the elegant lady detective would have acted. There was one woman who, whatever the opposition—knife-wielding psychopaths, poisonous snakes or rapidly rising tides—had everlastingly triumphed!

At least she was dressed for the part, she thought, smoothing a comforting hand over a taupe suede hip. Her tailored skirt had been teamed with an ivory silk shirt, which had deep lapels and splendidly full sleeves. On her feet she wore suede high heels, while a matching bag hung on her shoulder. Heavy gold chains had been fastened around her neck, and a gold stud was fixed in each ear. Her hair, which normally cascaded down her back in unruly raven-black curls, had been tamed into a burnished knot at the side of her head, and her make-up was meticulous.

Roxanne grinned. All this was well and good, but elegant ladies did not usually trundle push-chairs, she thought in amusement. Nor pop into the supermarket on their way to an assignation. Nor—she stopped to take a tissue from her bag—lick-wipe around the mouth of a blond eighteen-month-old imp who had yet to master the art of eating ice-cream and remaining impeccable.

'You've dropped some on your T-shirt, Barnaby,' she sighed, rubbing frantically at a besmirched Snoopy.

Her small son beamed, then made a sudden lunge at the tray beneath his seat. This past week he had discovered that when the push-chair was standing still, and if he reached far enough, he could with luck grab whatever groceries had been stored there—and throw them out. It was a great game.

Roxanne sat him up and straightened his white cotton sun-hat.

'No, you don't!'

A left was taken, and a right, and not much later they arrived at their destination—a small garden square. Looking around, her grey eyes opened wide in admiration. Four years ago Guy Slaney had occupied a bedsit in one of the shabbier districts of South London, but the heady rise in his career had brought about a correspondingly heady improvement in life-style. Chelsea included many charming villagey corners, and the square was one of the prettiest she had seen. In the centre, July sunshine dappled leafy plane trees which shaded a cut lawn, while on four sides ranged period-style houses with pillared porches and spotless white walls. Shiny black railings separated their flagged frontages from the road, and on each urns and tubs spilled with summer flowers—scarlet geraniums, pink Busy Lizzies, blue and white lobelia. On reaching the correct number, Roxanne saw that her quarry's home possessed the added distinction of a rambling rose, which hung fragrant yellow heads around his front door in glorious profusion. A grand house for a man who considered himself to be exceedingly grand! she thought disparagingly.

She opened the gate and negotiated the push-chair up over the step, but although she searched for a bell she could not find one. Lifting the lion's head on the brass knocker, Roxanne rapped smartly. There was no answer. She rapped again. Waited. Nothing. She pounded out a robust staccato tune. To no effect.

'He's out,' she sighed.

Barnaby bobbed a sage head. 'Out,' he repeated.

'But we'll be back tomorrow. And the next day. And the one after that if——'

She broke off. She had at last spied the bell, which was to one side of the porch and tucked behind the roses. Steering a careful finger between blossoms, leaves and branches, she pushed, but no corresponding ring sounded indoors. Was the bell broken? A second time she prodded, and tilted her head to listen, but all she heard was silence. She jabbed at the button. She experimented by jiggling it wildly from side to side. Roxanne pricked herself.

'Ouch!'

'Give it a rest, *please*,' a distant and dis-gruntled voice pleaded as she frowned at the evil-looking thorn which had embedded itself in her finger. 'If you're collecting for charity, come back later.'

Her recognition of the indoors protester was

instant. The son of a French mother and an English father, Guy Slaney had been provided, by the commingling of genes, with tawny Gallic colouring, Anglo-Saxon height, and a speech pattern which held an intriguing hint of *difference*. But Roxanne had no ear for the voice which had been likened to 'treacle poured over gravel'. Her immediate concern was removing the barb which jagged deep.

'I'm not,' she called, preoccupied.

'If you're selling something, I don't want any.'

'You've got it wrong.'

'Hack off!' he bellowed, exasperation peaking.

Hack off? Roxanne had not come across the expression before, but she had other priorities than the latest in abuse. Steeling herself, she nipped the thorn between two fingernails and, with a grimace and a second, more anguished ouch!, pulled it free. A hole gaped in the tender pad of her finger. A droplet of bright red blood began to swell.

'This is Roxanne,' she hollered, at last able to give him her concentration. 'Roxanne Dunn.'

There was silence.

'Who?' he shouted, and his voice sounded even fainter, as though, imagining she had gone—the gods be praised!—he had retreated to wherever it was that he had first come from.

She glared at the front door, at her bleeding finger, then swivelled to glare at a couple of schoolboys who, hearing the commotion, had stopped to listen. A few houses along, a window-cleaner hanging off his ladder made a third member of the audience. Why couldn't Guy Slaney be civilised and open up? She did not appreciate being forced to conduct a public conversation at tens of decibels, neither did she appreciate his lack of recognition. *Assignment Paris* might have been made a while ago, but people still stopped her in the street to reminisce about the mind-boggling horrors she had so serenely mastered. Yet the elevated Mr Slaney could not even remember her name!

'Roxanne Ledgard,' she corrected in a yell, belatedly acknowledging that he had known her before her marriage.

The identification resulted in the gradual approach of footsteps, some fumbling, and the ram of bolts being shot back. Eventually the door opened and a bleary-eyed man peered out.

'Rox. Hi,' he said, as though he had last seen her yesterday and not after a four-year gap. He yawned. 'Wadda you want?'

'I'd like to——' she began, then dried up abruptly, short of breath.

Guy Slaney had that drugged, heavy-headed, slightly dopey air which said she had wrenched him out of sleep and out of bed. Karen had been right, he was not pretty. His nose was too thin, his jaw too square, and his front teeth were crooked. Add brown-blond hair stuck up in tufts and dark stubble covering his jaw, and he looked rough, beat-up. Yet, wearing nothing but a brief pair of boxer-shorts, he struck her as dauntingly. . .physical. Roxanne gazed at him in surprise. His position on the step emphasised his six-feet-plus, but had he always been so broad-shouldered and well-muscled? With a tan which made his skin gleam, he reminded her of the kind of macho advertisement hunk who galloped bareback along beaches or crested cathedral waves on a surfboard. During the filming of *Assignment Paris* she had seen him in everyday clothes, jogging gear, a diver's outfit— even wearing a soft black leather suit which had clung in a way which left no doubt about his masculinity—but she had never seen him undressed.

'Yes?' he demanded, his tone making it plain that, although the greeting had been pleasant enough, patience came in short supply.

Roxanne pinned on a bright smile. 'Did I wake you? I'm sorry.'

'You would have awakened the dead!'

'I only knocked three times,' she protested.

'What about playing ten choruses of the Trumpet Voluntary on the bell?' he enquired.

She gave a shamefaced grin. 'It didn't seem to be working.'

'It is.'

The droplet of blood had begun to trickle. 'I've pricked my finger,' she said, sucking hard.

Guy scowled. 'What am I supposed to do, kiss it better?'

'You're supposed to prune your roses,' she retorted, rattled by his brusqueness. All she had done was cut short his sleep. She had not committed a heinous crime! If he chose to languish late and long between the sheets, recovering from some who-knew-what energy-sapping activity, how was she to know? 'I apologise for disturbing you, but——' ostentatiously she checked her watch '—it is eleven o'clock.'

Large fists were ground into his eyes. 'Eleven for you. However, my body clock's set at three a.m. Or some weird time.'

'You've been abroad?'

'I returned from Kenya yesterday.'

Roxanne experienced a twinge of remorse. Instead of carousing, he had been strapped in a seat for interminable hours, and after the long flight—possibly overnight—he must have been deeply asleep. Perhaps she should have telephoned first?

'Jet lag can be grim,' she sympathised.

'I feel as if there's an iron bar joining my ears together,' he replied curtly.

As he yawned again she recalled Karen's talk of how, after playing the highly praised second lead in one quality film, Guy Slaney had gone straight into another. Karen was her source of all such information—had to be, for she no longer owned a television nor splashed out on magazines.

'You were filming in Kenya?' Roxanne said conversationally.

'For the past fifteen weeks. What do you want?' Guy asked again.

'To speak to you—about the repeats of *Assignment Paris*.'

The acclaimed brown- and gold-flecked eyes narrowed. 'You know about that?'

Roxanne took the chance that his African stay would mean he had no idea of how much, or how little, had been publicised. And television companies had a penchant for plastering their activities—confidential or otherwise—over every available inch of news space.

'There was a mention in some paper or other,' she said offhandedly.

'Damn!' Guy sighed. 'Whatever you've read, the news is premature.'

Premature? Had Karen's informant got things wrong? Was he having second thoughts? Could those repeat fees be there for the taking, after all?

'You're not trying to veto the series?' she queried, swallowing down a smile.

'There's no "trying" involved. I *have* vetoed it.' He stretched, tanned arms lazily unfurling. 'Are you here to give thanks?'

Any thought of smiling vanished and Roxanne gaped, astonished that not only did he see nothing wrong in his high-handedness, but that he also expected her to be grateful.

'Thanks?' she repeated, nonplussed.

'Being associated with that trash was bad enough the first time around, but to go through it again——' Guy shuddered. '—you'd need to be a card-carrying masochist. The critics slated *Assignment Paris* right, left and centre, and with good reason. The storylines were non-existent, the dialogue was embarrassing, and a chimp with a rusty razor-blade seems to have been responsible for the editing,' he said, suddenly sounding remarkably articulate for someone half comatose. 'I figure that by keeping it off the screen I've done everyone a favour, not least the viewers.'

Roxanne's chin jutted. 'The television company must consider *Assignment Paris* has something going for it.'

'Maybe they do. Or maybe they've been let down with some other series and are desperate for a fill-in—desperate as in suicidal,' Guy remarked sardonically. He thrust her a suspicious glance. 'You're not saying you wouldn't have minded if it had been repeated, are you?'

'I would *love* it to be repeated,' she declared. 'I don't consider you've done anyone any favours.'

He gave an incredulous laugh. 'But the series came straight off the stable floor.'

'Good audience reaction is the criterion for a repeat, so it can't have been that bad!'

'Someone goofed with the viewing figures. The only people it could possibly have appealed to are those whose IQs do not exceed room temperature,' Guy carried on bruisingly.

'Then how come I received letters from businessmen, doctors, even a university don, telling me how much they'd enjoyed it?' Roxanne demanded.

'Sweetheart, what they enjoyed was you— *period*. You have the kind of face and figure——' the tiger eyes wandered down her body '—which make strong men buckle at the knees. Not only that, the camera loves you. OK, in *Assignment Paris* all you had to do was stand around and make mouths water, which you did to great effect, but why you didn't persevere and try to go on to something better, I don't know.' He scratched his stubbled jaw. 'Hell,' he said, in abrupt alarm, 'you're not responsible? You haven't been making noises to the TV blokes about resurrecting *Assignment Paris*? You're not hankering after a second slug of fame?'

'No, thanks,' she said crisply.

If the truth were told, what she *did* hanker for was for him to put on some clothes. Roxanne had no recollection of being disturbed by Guy Slaney's sexuality before, but today the sight of his golden shoulders, his firm-muscled torso, his scantily clad hips, was having an undeniable effect. Her pulse had accelerated. Her heart knocked. But why? Because he was the first near-nude young male she had seen in ages, she decided. Being in such close proximity with uncovered masculine flesh was an uncommon event, that was all.

'How about needing the publicity—some publicity!——' he jeered '—for a comeback?'

Roxanne shook a resolute head. 'You might be hooked on acting, but once was enough for me.'

'You think it has too much in common with warfare? Long periods of boredom punctuated by short bursts of terror,' Guy defined.

'I suppose it does,' she agreed, amused by the description, 'but it's not that. The thing which appalls me is the lack of——'

'Mickey!' Barnaby squealed all of a sudden, and pointed an excited finger at the boxer-shorts.

Guy shot a startled look downwards. 'What?'

'He's noticed the pattern. It's Mickey Mouse,' Roxanne explained.

'Oh. Yeah.' He gazed around as if he had only now realised he was providing her and her son, two schoolboys and a goggling window-cleaner with an intimate view of his underwear—though he did not seem bothered. Certainly he made no move to suggest that they should carry on their conversation indoors. 'You've caught me at a bad time,' Guy muttered, peering at the black-faced watch strapped to his wrist. 'I'm due out in half an hour.'

'Then you should be grateful I woke you,' she told him smartly.

'Is that so?' He nodded at the pushchair. 'I heard you have a child. What's he called?'

'Barnaby.'

The fierce looks she had been receiving melted into an engaging smile. 'Pleased to meet you, Barney.'

'I prefer Barnaby,' Roxanne said primly.

'And I prefer Barney, it's friendlier,' he said, coming down from the step to squat before the little boy. 'Hello, my name's Guy.'

His face and proffered hand were assessed with judge-like gravity.

'Guy,' Barnaby repeated, his grin indicating approval.

'You're sticky,' Guy complained as he formally shook the tiny fingers.

'I bought him an ice-cream on the way here. A chocolate one,' Roxanne added superfluously.

He straightened. 'I must buy Emma some chocolates when I go out,' he muttered. 'Daren't appear with nothing after all this time.'

Scared he might decide to go out immediately and leave *her* with nothing, Roxanne hastily steered the conversation back on track.

'Did it never occur to you that before giving *Assignment Paris* the thumbs down there were other people who needed to be consulted?' she enquired.

'Needed to be consulted?' He held the phrase out in mental tweezers and inspected it. 'No.'

'No?' Roxanne shrilled, horrified by such arrogance.

Guy Slaney *was* a talented actor, she thought derisively. The best. Four years ago she had believed him to be modest, reasonable, considerate of his fellow men—but all this had been exposed as pretence. The only person who featured in his scheme of things was Big Noise himself!

'No. You see——'

'You appear to be suffering from an identification crisis!' Roxanne exploded, forgetting all about that mental memo not to lose her temper. 'Everyone else regards you as just another mortal, but you think you're God!'

His full mouth thinned. 'It isn't like that.'

'Dead right!' she snapped. 'You're not God, you're a world-class slug! Apart from me, there must be twenty or thirty other people who appeared in the series at one time or another and, as everyone knows, ninety per cent of actors are out of work ninety per cent of the time. What about their repeat fees?' she demanded furiously. 'Don't you think they might have welcomed them, or don't you care?'

'I care,' Guy rasped, with a glance at his watch which advised that, as he had little tolerance for

her attack, he also had little time. 'Though I
should like to point out that because *Assignment
Paris* was a low-budget production, the fees
were on the low side, too, so whatever the
supporting actors miss out on, they're not miss-
ing out on much.' He rubbed his fingertips
across his chest, drawing her eyes to the whorls
of dark gold hair. Roughly inscribing an inverted
triangle, the hair tapered as his chest tapered
into his waist, becoming a strip which plunged
vertically down over his stomach and into his
shorts. 'However, the reason I regret the premature leakage is that before the news became
public there were things I'd hoped to do, one of
which being to discover whether any of our ex-
associates are down on their luck and, if so,
make a bona fide payment. There, now that you
know the other actors won't be going hungry,
are you satisfied?'

Roxanne frowned. 'To a point, but——'

'To a point?' Guy protested, as though he had
expected her to fall to her knees in gratitude and
admiration.

'Yes, but although the fees were poor, you, I
and——' she paused, summoning up the name
of the elderly bachelor who had played the third
main role '—Brian Cottrell received a reasonable
sum, and would do so from a repeat. I dare say
Brian won't be too happy when he learns he's
expected to forgo his fees. Or——' she watched

him keenly '—will you be recompensing him, too?'

'No.'

'Why not?' she demanded.

'Because he died last March. And as far as me axing *Assignment Paris* goes, Brian would have given three cheers. He'd done some fine work in his time; no way would he have wanted a rerun of that as his epitaph!'

'I'm sure he wouldn't have minded,' Roxanne declared. She took a breath. 'Don't you think it would have been polite to have consulted *me* about the repeats?'

Guy checked the time again. 'Polite to advise you of my intention, yes—and I'd planned to do that. But if by "consult" you mean ask your permission—no. Why should I, when the right of veto is written into the contract?'

She blinked. 'A veto's written—written in?' she faltered.

'It's a standard clause.'

'You mean you have the option to stop any repeats?'

He nodded. 'And so do you, and so did Brian. When you signed on the dotted line you agreed to all this,' he said, flinging her an impatient look. 'If you don't believe me, check your own small print.'

Everything took a downward spiral. This was a blow she had never anticipated, not once considered. Too late, Roxanne realised she should not just have telephoned before confronting him, she should have also checked out a few facts. So Guy Slaney *did* have the right to block a rerun, and to block the fees she had so fondly imagined would be hers.

'The show made some people happy before, and it could do again,' she declared, in a desperate stab at recovery and a renewed attempt at persuasion.

'It could also do untold damage to my career,' he retorted.

'Twaddle!'

'I stand in awe of your gift for blind certainty,' Guy replied, his tone a millimetre on the right side of the knife-edge between politeness and punch-throwing irritation, 'but, after working for the past ten years to become an overnight success, I've reached the point where what happens now can seriously affect what happens to the rest of my career. In acting it's difficult to control your own destiny, but I intend to control it as much as I can—which means I won't be giving the go-ahead to the second run of a piece of work which I heartily wish I could obliterate.'

'You consider it diminishes you?' Roxanne demanded.

'I know it'll restrict me!'

'I don't agree.'

He lambasted her with a look. 'That's because you were in and out of acting so fast, you haven't a clue what I'm talking about. And, what's more, you have no intention of listening. Why are you so keen on the series being shown again?' Guy demanded. 'I assumed you'd come here crusading on behalf of the supporting actors, but there's more to it than that.' Eyes leery, he studied her, then he slapped the flat of his hand hard against his thigh, making her jump. 'I know what it is. You want your own damn fees!'

Roxanne's pang of dismay was hotly pursued by resentment. She had hoped to soft-pedal on her true interest, skip over any mention of personal gain, and now the admission came hard.

'So?' she said, head held high.

'So you're the widow of Hamish Dunn, the well-known impresario and backer of shows. A man who invested millions in the theatre. A man who made millions. A man who died two years ago and left all those millions——' Guy jabbed an accusatory finger '—to you!'

CHAPTER TWO

ROXANNE refused to be browbeaten. 'That doesn't make one iota of difference,' she retorted.

'No?' Guy uttered an expletive. 'This morning you've dragged me out of bed, you've called me names, you've done your utmost to batter me into submission, and for what?' His nostrils dilated with disgust. 'A sum of money which, to you, represents loose change!'

'We're talking about thousands of pounds,' she protested.

His eyes scraped over her, advising he knew that her jewellery had been fashioned from twenty-four-carat gold and that her clothes bore the tags of top designers.

'What we're talking about,' he said scathingly, 'is a young woman who can't bear the thought of a nought-point-one addition to her bank account passing her by—and that's all there'd be left of the fees once you'd paid top-bracket tax.' The boxer-shorts, which had taken a dangerous slide, were hitched higher up his hips. 'I imagined that when I contacted you and explained you'd——' He broke off. 'What the hell does it matter what I imagined? I was wrong. It seems I've been wrong about you all along.' He gave a harsh laugh. 'And to think I defended you when you married Hamish Dunn. I told everyone——'

'The money a person earns from their own endeavours is totally different from money someone else has provided,' Roxanne interrupted, fearful of what he might say next.

She knew precisely what it was that Guy had defended her against—the gossips who, often carelessly of her presence, had uncharitably speculated on the attraction a girl in her twenties could find in a man old enough to be her father. That Hamish, with his swept-back silver hair and dashing style, had been immensely likeable had not seemed to matter. His highly publicised wealth had.

Guy arched a sardonic brow. 'Is that right?'

'Yes. Your own money has a special significance. It bestows pride. Independence.' She saw her words were falling on stony ground. 'If you were a woman, you'd understand.'

'But I'm not. And although you earned the money the first time around,' he said silkily, 'the second time would have counted as pure baksheesh.'

Ready to protest, Roxanne decided otherwise. Another pointed look at his watch had emphasised what she already knew—her opponent was in no mood to respond to friendly persuasion, or a battering, or whatever.

'I'll come back another time,' she said, 'and we can talk about this again.'

Guy uttered a low growl of frustration. 'There's nothing to talk about!' She made no comment. 'What do you do all day?' he asked as she released the brake on the pushchair.

'I care for my son.'

'No nanny?'

'None. And, for the record, no butler, cook or daily help, either,' Roxanne told him, refusing to be classified as a pampered layabout.

His brows rose. 'You look after that huge place in Belgravia with—what, a billiard-room, a library and six or seven bedrooms, single-handed?'

'No, no, the house was far too grand, not to my taste at all, so we moved,' she said airily. 'To a flat a couple of miles from here.'

'Which is smaller?'

'More manageable.'

'So you have free time?' he said, his eyes locking with hers.

Roxanne swallowed. All of a sudden the 'tiger' label seemed awesomely apt. Controlled and watchful, his look contained a hint of ferocity which warned that, if she did not take care, he could spring and grab her by the throat.

'Some,' she agreed warily.

'Then, if you're so keen on having your *own* money, why don't you find yourself a job?' Guy enquired.

'Because, as I've just said, I care for my son.'

'Plenty of other women who have kids go out to work.'

'Barnaby is a tiny child who never knew his father, and now you're advocating that his mother should desert him, too?' she protested. 'And if I did dump him with a baby minder, what line would you suggest I try?' she questioned, her voice tart. 'Apart from my one attempt at acting, all I've ever done is model, but I'm twenty-seven and I've been out of action for ages, and——' she fixed on the root of her objection '—modelling is unpredictable.'

Guy took a step backwards on to the porch. 'I've noticed a hamburger joint on the King's Road which is always wanting staff. "No experience necessary" the advertisement says.' A broad shoulder rested against one of the white pillars. 'Waitressing would be regular, why not give it a spin?'

Roxanne gritted her teeth. There he lounged—the man with all the questions, all the answers, all the power. The man who was witholding cash which had so nearly been hers. *Hers.* And now, although his hands were not around her throat, he had trapped her—or thought he had.

'Right, I will,' she announced, mutinous urge combining with retaliatory tactic. She hooked her bag on her shoulder and unlatched the gate. 'I'll apply for a job *now!*'

'Whoa,' he objected as she stepped on to the pavement. 'You're not thinking of leaving Barney with me?'

'As you're the one who's so keen on me finding work, you can look after him while I'm gone. I shouldn't be more than an hour.'

Guy's face fell. 'But you can't! I mean, I can't,' he implored, gazing at her across the railings. 'I'm going out. You know I am. It's important. And I'm late already.'

'Then you'll need to be a little later,' she informed him sweetly. 'Like sixty minutes.'

'But——'

Roxanne raised a hand and wiggled her fingers. 'Enjoy,' she smiled, and strode away.

For the past half-hour, the girls behind the counter had been dealing out hamburgers and french fries with the speed of card-sharps. Roxanne admired their professionalism, she applauded their energy, but she could not see herself serving fast-food decked out in an unceasing smile, a bow-tie and a cocked hat. Wedged at a corner table with three ravenously eating, raucously chattering secretaries, she swallowed down dregs of cold coffee. Right now, she could not see herself persuading Guy Slaney that *Assignment Paris* should be rerun, either. But the money he had hijacked could be vital to her life—and Barnaby's. Granted, the hair-tearing stage had yet to be reached. Not only was there a roof over their heads, but she also possessed the means of acquiring sums of cash. Instinctively her fingers went to her gold chains. Yet over the months those means had been dwindling and, no matter how carefully or how thinly she spread them, were, in time, destined to run out. Roxanne straightened her spine. Feebleness had never ranked among her characteristics, and she refused to be feeble now. Guy considered the subject closed, but so what? She would make another attempt to retrieve those fees. She must.

Yet what could she do—reveal that, far from being loose change, the money would be used for essential, day-to-day living expenses? She gave her head a little shake. At the time of Hamish's death she had vowed that the errors of the past, and their consequences, would remain nobody's business but her own, and she had no intention of making a grand confession now. Even Karen, who knew things had gone badly wrong, had not received an explanation, and she would be spilling no beans to an airs-and-graces actor—even if he did believe her to be a grasping gold-digger. Roxanne stared down into the empty plastic cup. Today Guy Slaney had merely added his name to the long list of those who regarded her with acute suspicion, but the censure still hurt. She had never been able to thicken her skin and ignore the slurs.

Fractiously, she tugged at a wisp of dark hair

which curled beside her ear. Guy had maintained that she did not know enough about his profession to understand what he was talking about, but what was there to understand? In acting you won some, you lost some. It was inevitable. Few, if any, could claim an unblemished career, so what made him so pernickety? Admittedly, *Assignment Paris* had been. . . second-class, but for most people television went in one eye and out the other, so what did it matter?

Realising that the secretaries were ready to depart, Roxanne also left the restaurant. Her stated hour's absence might still have twenty minutes to go, but she was eager to reclaim Barnaby. The King's Road, so-called because in days gone by it had been the royal route from the palace of Whitehall to Hampton Court, was a Mecca for seekers of with-it fashions, and past trendy boutiques and jazzy shoe shops she went, threading her way through the crowds. As she turned into a quieter street her pace quickened. The sooner she and her son were reunited, the better. Roxanne began to jog. Unconsciously, the jog increased to a run, and by the time she reached the rose-garlanded door she was panting and sweaty-browed. It took a minute to catch her breath and refix the knot of hair which was on the verge of collapsing, then she rang the bell.

Although Guy had insisted it worked, as

before she could hear no accompanying sound. She made herself wait a respectable time, and tried it again. After four tries, and four waits, Roxanne was ready to scream—or break a window. Instead she lifted the lion's head knocker.

'Won't do no good, darlin',' the window-cleaner said, ambling past with his bucket and cloth. 'He went out. With the little boy.'

Barnaby wasn't here? He had been whisked off to some other place? A primal mother's urge to be with her child screamed inside her. She needed to know her son was safe. She needed to see him, *now*.

'You all right?' enquired the window-cleaner when she raised a distressed hand to her head.

'Yes. Thanks,' she mumbled, and, reassured by her smile, he carried on his way.

Roxanne sagged against a white pillar. On the rare occasions when she had left the little boy it had been for a good reason, and then he had been secure at home with someone he knew—like Mrs Ashby from downstairs, or one of the Hussein children—yet today, on a whim, she had abandoned him to a man he had never seen before! Despite the heat, she shivered. What she had done frightened her. How could she have given that flippant wave and sauntered away? Whatever had possessed her to ditch him? It made no sense. It was downright irresponsible! She knew that she was worried about the future, but until now she had never realised *how* worried.

Seeing her disappear, had Barnaby begun to sob? Roxanne wondered. Had he been sobbing ever since? Was he sobbing now? As she imagined his little face puckered up and fat tears rolling down his cheeks, tears brimmed in her own eyes. He was barely more than a baby, but could this be his fate—to be deposited with strangers? If the money she spent so cautiously ran out, then yes. She would be forced to leave him in order to earn their living. A lump formed in her throat. If she surrendered Barnaby day after day after day, not only would they miss each other, but they would miss out on that all-important bonding. Roxanne gulped. More than anything else in the world she wanted her son to grow up happy and confident and rounded, which meant she wanted him to spend his first precious years with her—not being stashed in this place and that like an unwanted parcel.

Walking to the corner of the square, she peered left and right, but only a few anonymous people were in sight. Roxanne nibbled unhappily at a fingernail. If only she could remember more about Guy Slaney—like his attitude towards children! Yet, despite racking her brains, all she could dredge up was the vague memory of a young man who had done his best to help her gauche attempts at acting, a young man full of everyday agreeability, yet a young man who, when the director had made yet another lacklustre decision, had finally lost his temper and shouted. Consternation held her motionless. Admittedly, on that occasion Guy had had just cause for losing his temper, but perhaps he would consider a yelling toddler just cause, too? Presumably Barnaby had accompanied him on his visit to the chocolate-eating Emma, but if *Assignment Paris* was reckoned to be bad for his image, what chance had a bawling, red-faced, runny-nosed child? Intent on a reunion—and after nearly four months apart it would be impassioned—Guy and his girlfriend would not require Barnaby to play gooseberry, no matter how he behaved. Roxanne's throat constricted. Had he been parked in a room all alone? A gloomy one?

The next ten minutes dragged by like ten years, and when the hour was up and her son failed to appear Roxanne felt as if she were ageing a year each minute, too. Where was Barnaby? Why the delay? What brainstorm had had her entrusting her beloved child to a near stranger? When, eventually, a shape in the distance focused itself into—yes, thank heavens, yes!—the returning duo, she galloped to meet them.

'Everything all right?' she demanded, wide grey eyes moving over her son like anxious searchlights. But there were no tears, and no tell-tale signs of past distress; on the contrary, he seemed to glow with an almost smug contentment.

'Everything's fine,' Guy replied, then added cryptically, 'He's had a smashing time.'

'Smashing?' Roxanne repeated, alert to the implication. Like all toddlers, Barnaby was inquisitive, eager to touch everything—and clumsy. After a couple of breakages she had learned her lesson and placed all ornaments at the flat safely beyond his reach, but now she had visions of shattered vases, splintered glass, him grabbing a china figurine and flinging it down. 'How do you mean?' she asked, taut with apprehension.

'We were waiting to cross the road when suddenly a woman alongside squealed and clutched at her ankle. I looked down and—what do you know?—there was buddy boy tossing out eggs from beneath the pushchair as fast as he could go. He plastered her tights in egg-white and biffed a Yorkshire Terrier on the nose. I tried to stop him, or at least catch the eggs which came next, but you could have made an omelette from the ones he lobbed out into the traffic. Which is why we're late. I've been pacifying the wounded and——' Guy raised a supermarket bag '—buying replacements.'

So that was what 'smashing' meant! Roxanne kept her expression determinedly stiff-lipped and grave. To her the story sounded funny, but experience had shown that the male of the

species, especially those who risk being recognised, could resent involvement in undignified
behaviour—and it seemed doubtful that his
sense of humour would stretch to crawling in
the gutter. She said a fervent prayer that no
photographer had been around. The aim had
been to beguile Guy Slaney, not antagonise him,
and a candid-camera shot in tomorrow's news-
papers would completely wreck her campaign.

'I'm very sorry,' she said, loading her apology
with as much humble pie as it would carry.

'Not as sorry as I was.'

Hearing a satirical lilt to his voice, Roxanne
sneaked a look. The corners of his eyes had
crinkled. His mouth had tweaked. Guy was
grinning!

'There I was on my hands and knees,' he
continued, 'with a shrieking female on one side
and a hysterical dog on the other, fielding eggs
as if I played cricket for England.'

Now she could laugh. Whether it was how he
told the tale, or gratitude that he did not find
the episode degrading, or relief at finding
Barnaby unscathed, Roxanne did not know—
but mirth bubbled out of her like champagne.

'It sounds hilarious,' she gasped.

'Slapstick comedy,' Guy agreed. 'And right in
the middle of it a girl thrust a book under my
nose and asked for an autograph.' He guffawed
with laughter. 'After the reply she received, I
doubt she'll be so hot on me any more.'

Roxanne summoned up her strictest voice. 'That was naughty,' she told Barnaby, but a smile slid out to spoil the effect, and she was not surprised when the little boy looked back at her from beneath his sun-hat and giggled. She turned to Guy. 'Thanks for buying more eggs. Let me pay you.'

'Well, did you get it?' he demanded, as she handed over the money.

'Get what? Oh, the job.' She gazed at a point somewhere beyond his left shoulder. 'No. The manager was on holiday, so——'

'Rox, we both know you haven't applied to become a waitress and never intended to,' he interrupted in exasperation. 'What I'm talking about is your contract. Did you go home and find it, and check out that what I said was true? You didn't appear to believe me,' he grated when she frowned.

'I do. It's just that—well, I don't have my contract any more. I cleared out a whole pile of papers some time back and——'

'You threw it away,' Guy completed when she made an aimless gesture. 'It's obvious you never expected *Assignment Paris* to see the light of day again!'

'I disposed of the document by accident,' Roxanne said defensively.

'Did you now? Then I guess you'd better see mine.' He set off walking with the pushchair. 'Come along.'

'There's no need,' she protested, hurrying alongside.

He flung her a glance. 'If I'm to get you off my back, there's every need. I doubt you'd have landed a job peddling burgers,' he remarked as they went down the street. 'You're too well-dressed. One look and they'd have decided you were far too grand a dame to ever——'

'What about you?' Roxanne cut in, miffed by the description. Maybe she was being oversensitive, yet 'too grand a dame' seemed to run disagreeably parallel with 'rich and greedy widow'. 'As I remember it, all you ever wore off camera were jeans and a sweatshirt, but——' a wave of her hand indicated his cream silk shirt, neatly knotted tie, smart dark trousers, '——look at you now.'

'I'm not usually so formal,' Guy said, pushing back the hair which fell over his brow. In the interval since she had last seen him he had shaved and shampooed, and his hair had become a glossy bronze helmet which curled around his ears and at the nape of his neck. 'It's just that Emma's a stickler for a correct code of dress. Once I visited her in an open-necked shirt and she almost went berserk.'

'She sounds like Hamish. He used to complain bitterly about men without ties. Reckoned they were sloppy. I told him he was out of date, that——' Abruptly aware of sounding disloyal,

Roxanne changed direction. 'How old is Emma?' she asked.

'Eighty.' He grinned at her look of bewilderment. 'I'm not her toy-boy—heaven forbid! She's the mother of a friend of mine, a lighting designer. Two years ago he went to live in the States and, as she doesn't have any other family and he said she didn't have any friends, I offered to keep an eye on her. I soon discovered why she lacks friends,' he said drily. 'She's the sourest old bird I've ever met. Apparently she felt she'd married beneath her, so her marriage was one long fight interspersed with stony silences, and as the years passed by she became more and more embittered. She lives in a home for the elderly by the river and is well looked after, but she never has a good word to say for anyone—and especially not men. I'm criticised on every visit—for what I say, what I wear, what I do.'

'Yet you continue to go?'

'Crazy, isn't it?' Guy said as they turned into the square.

Roxanne did not consider him crazy; she thought he was kind—and a more complex character than she had imagined. Although she had never actively subscribed to the idea that actors were shallow creatures, she had to admit this demonstration of social conscience surprised her.

'What was Emma's reaction to your taking Barnaby?' she queried.

They had reached his house. Guy hoicked the pushchair under the porch and unlocked the front door, then stood aside for her to enter the hall.

'Amazingly for a woman who'd previously shown all the warmth of an iceberg, it was unadulterated joy. Even if he did yank out her hearing-aid and knock over somebody's walking-frame.'

'Oh, dear!'

'Don't worry. One smile and buddy boy here gets away with murder.' He bent to tickle Barnaby, who went off into fits of giggles. 'When we left, all the old people and most of the staff fought to kiss him goodbye.' Guy conjured up a piteous expression. 'It's never happened to me.'

Roxanne grinned. 'For which I imagine you're eternally grateful?'

'You imagine right. Speaking of kisses, how's the finger?'

She held it up. 'Better, apart from a hole.'

'A hole?' Guy exclaimed in mock horror. He winked at Barnaby, who giggled anew. 'The remedy for that must be a big kiss.'

As he grabbed hold of her hand and pressed his lips to the offending finger, Roxanne stood very still. His performance might be for her son's benefit, but Guy's casual invasion of her personal space, the feel of his mouth on her skin, was making her pulse race again. And this time he wore clothes—so much for the theory that her earlier problem had been with his nudity!

'More,' giggled Barnaby when Guy released her hand.

He grinned. 'What d'you think, Rox? Do I work my way along the rest of your fingers, or——' his eyes fell to her mouth '—concentrate on something else?'

Roxanne drew in a shaky breath. All of a sudden, the air had become supercharged. Was he joking. . .or not? Should she dismiss the question as light-hearted banter, or should she take him seriously? Those brown and gold eyes *looked* serious. But. . .But. . .It was so long since she had been caught up in any male-female by-play that she did not know what to think—or what to do.

By leaning forward and kissing her on the lips, Guy took the decision from her. His kiss was light—not much more than a dab—but it was the first she had had in two years. Roxanne's heart began to hammer. She had never paid any thought to his French ancestry before, yet now his easy confidence struck her as infinitely Gallic. With a smile playing around his mouth and an amused look in his brown eyes, Guy possessed a disturbing air of sexual *savoir-faire*.

'More?' he enquired when she continued to stand there.

'No!'

'It was that bad?'

'No.' Roxanne went pink. 'I mean. . .'

She needed a slick answer. Or two. Or three. Feverishly her mind was frisked, but slick answers were not to be found.

'Birdie!' Barnaby carolled, and she was saved.

Through an open door and across a room, the little boy had spotted a chaffinch outside the window.

'Suppose Barney has a run round in the garden while I show you the contract?' Guy suggested.

With a hasty nod, she bent and unstrapped her son from his pushchair.

'You're very lucky to have a garden,' Roxanne said wistfully.

'You don't?'

'No, the flat's on the third floor and doesn't even have a balcony. It's not the ideal place for bringing up a child. Still,' she continued, helping Barnaby out, 'we go to the park every day, so we get by.'

After the splendid exterior of the house, the dingy hall had been a disappointment, but as she followed her host through his living-room her eyes swung from acid-yellow walls to heavy maroon velvet curtains to a plastic-topped bar in the corner. Roxanne gave a silent groan. An interest in interior design meant that she entered other people's homes hopeful of finding clever furnishing ideas, a combination of unexpected colours, new fabric designs—but this room offered nothing. Bluntly, it was a disaster. And the sad thing was that the deft use of a paint-brush, lighter curtains, and a few imaginative touches could transform it entirely. Spacious, south-facing, and with french windows which opened out on to a paved patio and grassy oval beyond, it possessed great potential.

Guy opened the french doors. 'Want to——?' he began, but already the little boy was outside.

Across the flagstones and on to the grass he scampered, as fast as his chubby legs would carry him. A wonderland awaited. The finch had flown away, but he didn't notice for there were butterflies to chase and upturned plant-pots to investigate and an old watering-can which could be carted around. As she watched him dash from one delight to the next, Roxanne smiled. Barnaby loved to play outdoors and here, unlike in the park, he could run free. Nothing in the walled garden could be spoiled, for the grass was overgrown and the borders were thick with weeds.

'It'll be respectable by the winter,' Guy said, following her eyes. 'My next job's a play here in London, so I'll have time to get to grips. Unless, of course, we open and close on the first night, in which case it'll be back to the market-place looking for employment.' For a moment he was silent, then he roused himself. 'The study's this way.'

Going with him along the hall, there were glimpses of dark brown paintwork, peeling wall-paper, an old-fashioned kitchen with scuffed linoleum.

'What made you buy this place?' Roxanne asked curiously.

'It was midway between a Chinese take-away and the launderette, which solved half of life's problems, and as I don't run a car its proximity to the underground solved the other fifty per cent,' he replied, and grinned. 'Abysmal, isn't it?'

'The outside's lovely,' good manners made her say.

'That's because the residents' association lays down rules. An old Armenian bloke owned it, and when he died and it came to the sale his daughter chucked in light fittings, furniture, the lot. At the time I regarded the extras as a bonus, but now——' Guy gave a deep-throated chuckle '—now I realise she was simply avoiding paying for everything to be scrapped.'

'How long have you lived here?' Roxanne enquired as they entered a study lined with floor-to-ceiling shelves, which were jam-packed with dusty books.

'I moved in a year ago, though I've only managed to spend a total of three months in residence. That's why I haven't had time to do anything. Mind you, as well as not having time I don't have much money. I'm up to my ears in mortgage repayments. However, I'm saving as hard as I can.' He pulled open the top drawer of a filing cabinet and placed a document on the desk. 'Read on.'

Her eyes went to the contract and the paragraph he indicated. There it was in black and white—a clause which gave each of the main actors the right to reject a repeat of the series after a lapse of two years, if they so wished. There was no need for Guy to make payments to anyone and, she acknowledged, in his position most people would not have bothered.

'Thanks.' Roxanne straightened, took a deep breath, and looked him in the eye. 'However, I don't consider a contract to be the issue here. For someone who's reckoned to be the smartest kid on the acting block, a rerun isn't going to——'

He made a low sound of annoyance. 'Couldn't you at least attempt to see things from my side?'

'Couldn't you at least attempt to keep a sense of proportion?' she retaliated.

'I am.'

'No, you're not!' Having praised him as the 'smartest kid' and been ignored, Roxanne was in no mind to waste her breath on praise again. 'I realise there's an actor's ego strutting around inside you, but——'

Guy thrust the contract back into its slot and slammed shut the drawer. 'If you're going to address me like a public meeting again, don't bother. And don't bother to hold your breath until the fateful day when I agree to a rerun, because it's not going to happen.'

Her stomach plunged. The pronouncement sounded horribly final.

'Never?'

'Life can be hell, can't it?' he said laconically.

And how! she thought.

'You have this desire for your own money, but what would you spent it on?' Guy asked. Disdainful eyes looked her up and down. 'Even more new clothes?'

'Everything I'm wearing is three years old,' Roxanne informed him curtly.

'All the more reason to buy something different,' he drawled. 'Perhaps some seductive low-cut outfits to entice rich husband Number Two?'

She balled her fists. 'There won't be another husband, rich or otherwise,' she declared.

'From now on you intend to go it alone?'

'I do,' she said, and marched out of the study and back to the living-room.

Through the french windows she saw Barnaby happily filling a plant-pot with soil. His hands were black, as were his T-shirt and shorts. The minute they were home, she would need to put him in the bath. Still, at least *he* had gained something from today, Roxanne thought wryly.

'Isn't it possible that your memory of *Assignment Paris* could be distorted?' Guy said as he joined her. 'How many episodes did you see?'

'Not all of them,' she replied, shying away from the admission that she had watched only two. 'The series was shown at a time when— when I had more to interest me than sitting at home in front of the television.'

He lifted a brow. 'You were being courted by the man whom the papers christened the "modern-day Midas"? It was a dizzy round of candle-lit dinners, weekends in Rome, visits to the furriers to select mink jackets?'

'Wrong—on all points!' Roxanne slammed, her grey eyes blazing. 'One, I hadn't met Hamish at that point, Two, not everything he touched turned to gold. He did put money into shows which flopped. Three, I've never been to Rome. And four, I wouldn't wear real fur.'

Silenced by her outburst, Guy frowned. 'Suppose you take another look at *Assignment Paris*?' he suggested. 'I can arrange it with the television people.'

'I'd rather you arranged for the nation to have another look,' Roxanne replied doggedly. 'I think you're taking the repeats far too——'

Tanned hands were raised. 'Pack it in,' Guy ordered. 'I've had enough. Gather up Barney and leave. I'm going back to bed!'

CHAPTER THREE

AT LONG last Barnaby had fallen asleep. With a sigh of relief, Roxanne tiptoed out of the room and closed the door. If they had been alone in the flat, she could have drawn the bedclothes up around her ears and ignored his middle-of-the-night playing, but they were not. Salim Hussein was here on yet another visit, and she could not allow his rest to be broken by what had threatened to be an endless run of loud, reverberating raspberries. Where her son had heard the spluttering noises and learned how to make them, she could not imagine—but she ardently wished he would forget!

Back in bed, she seemed to have barely nodded off again before Salim was pounding on the door.

'Wake! Wake!' he called, in his strongly accented English. 'It is the time to arise.'

Roxanne pushed a tangle of dark hair from her eyes and squinted at the clock. It was almost nine; she had slept through the alarm! Thrusting her feet into fluffy mules and her arms into a pale pink satin wrap, she headed for the bath-room. A quick wash, clean of teeth, brush of hair, and she sped to the kitchen. Ten minutes later, she and the young Arab were eating breakfast.

'I'm afraid you're going to be late for college,' she apologised as she poured his coffee.

He smiled a dazzling white smile. 'Please, do not worry.'

'You seem cheerful this morning,' Roxanne remarked. 'Are you feeling better?'

'Yes, thanks to you. Those pills you gave me were miraculous. Ten minutes after I had. . .' Salim hesitated, seeking her confirmation that he was choosing the right verb and the correct tense '. . .swallowed?' She nodded. 'Swallowed them, my sore head vanished and I fell into a deep sleep.'

'Headache vanished,' she corrected.

'Headache. It is such a comfort to travel to a foreign land and find you here so willing to help me,' he went on earnestly. 'I am in your debt. And my brother is in your debt. And my sisters. We venerate your patience and your friendship.'

Roxanne became busy buttering her toast. Although the Arabic way tended towards verbal extravagance, Salim constantly went over the top. Yesterday evening his praise of her provision of two simple aspirin had been elaborate and long, and now all it needed was the slightest encouragement and she knew he would gush more torrents of stilted-English gratitude. Yet, although she had cooked and washed and cared for all four Hussein offspring during their various visits over the past year, it was she who had the most cause to be grateful—to their father.

It had been shortly after Hamish's funeral when Mohammed Hussein had approached her with a generous offer to purchase the flat.

'For me it would be an investment pure and simple,' her husband's long-time crony had explained, waving a bejewelled hand, 'so if you agree, and if it would suit you to continue living here, please do. You would be helping me by keeping the property cared for and used.'

As debts had begun to surface like hungry sharks, his suggestion had come as a godsend, yet Roxanne's relief had been strongly peppered with suspicion. Not knowing the Arab well, she had wondered about his motives. Presumably he had, somehow, realised her financial state, so was he providing free accommodation as a kindly gesture to the widow of a friend—or did the offer come with strings attached? She hated to be cynical, but the past few years had taught her that things were rarely as 'pure and simple' as they seemed. Any interest Mr Hussein had shown in her thus far had been platonic, yet she had not been able to help wondering if, once she was in his debt, the situation might change. Whenever he visited London he left his wife at home, so could he be planning an extramarital adventure? Might his genial exterior conceal a lascivious streak?

After much agonising, Roxanne had accepted his offer. Not only had she been in desperate need of money but, being four months pregnant, her basic urge had been to stay put. She had, however, been wary of outstaying her welcome, and, although her benefactor clearly regarded the property as a long-term investment, she had insisted that whenever he wished her to depart he need only say.

'My brother will give me a home until I get fixed up elsewhere,' she had informed him.

When the deeds had first changed hands, she had been on pins. Was Mr Hussein going to arrive, move into the spare bedroom, and move in on her? Her waistline had expanded, though not by so much, and some men preferred their women on the plump side, didn't they? But as time had rolled by and his contact had remained undeviatingly neutral and brief, her fears had vanished. His kindness came from the heart—alleluia!

Barnaby had been six months old when a chance remark had shown her a way to pay back her landlord's generosity, if only in a small part.

'Had I not had a good grounding in English, I would never have been able to enjoy Hamish's friendship,' the portly Arab had mused during an infrequent phone call. 'I suppose it's time my children brushed up on the language.'

Immediately Roxanne had offered to seek out a suitable school and provide hospitality. And when in due course Fatima, the elder daughter, had arrived, she had made delicious meals, played tourist-guide, spent evening after evening listening to the recital of grammar rules, verbs, vocabulary. As a result the teenager had returned home so pleased with her stay and so fluent after the intensive eight-week course that in double-quick time the second daughter had appeared—and later the two sons had landed. Like his sisters, the younger one had come top of the class, but Salim had struggled. The eldest of the brood showed little aptitude for learning. Yet if he lagged behind in brainpower, when it came to good looks he ran ahead of the field. Tall, slim and blessed with thick black hair and the darkest, most outrageously long-lashed eyes, he was a beautiful young man. Whenever he walked down the street, all heads turned. Mr Hussein, however, had no interest in his son and heir's visual appeal—what mattered was his English, and the pidgin variety was not good enough. Salim must try again. And again.

'Time for you to go,' Roxanne declared as her guest drained his cup. She waited for him to collect his jacket and briefcase, then opened the front door. 'Got everything?' she asked.

'Yes, thank you. And thank you for the relief last night. I appreciate it. I appreciate all that you do for me.'

'My pleasure,' she muttered, ushering him out on to the landing. The reluctant student's first lesson would be well under way. She had no intention of allowing him to miss the second.

'You make me feel so good,' Salim declared as he pulled open the door to the passenger lift. 'You are so good.'

Roxanne flashed a smile. 'I try.'

'I'll see you this evening. I look forward to your. . .services?'

'Yes, yes,' she said, more interested in getting rid of him than in straightening out his English. 'Phew!' she sighed as the lift began its descent.

Roxanne tightened the sash of her wrap and turned. Now she would wash the breakfast pots, make the beds and, at last, get dressed.

'Interesting,' a low voice murmured as she stepped towards her front door.

Startled, she spun round—and found Guy Slaney standing at the top of the stairs on the far side of the landing. Hands in his pockets and sneakered feet crossed, he was leaning against the wall. The open lift door must have masked his presence, but how had he got in? she wondered. One of the advantages of living in the mansion block was its security. Before anyone could gain entrance at the main door, they had to buzz the flat they required and state their identity. Mrs Ashby had probably been leaving as he arrived, she decided, and had unethically granted him admission. Her middle-aged neighbour had a weakness for athletic young men, and Guy looked staggeringly fit and healthy. Roxanne frowned. What he did *not* look like was an actor—especially one who, so Karen had claimed, was a legend in embryo. Indeed, in faded Levis and open-throated shirt, he looked determinededly *un*theatrical, *un*glamorous.

'What are you doing here?' she demanded, surprise crisping her tone.

'Visiting.'

'Visiting me?'

'Yes. I got your address from the phone book.' Guy walked forward. 'Why so surprised? You obviously have other gentlemen visitors. Enthusiastic ones.'

'Salim's English goes off course at times,' she said, her mind flying to the scene he must have witnessed. She gave a hasty smile. 'All that talk of services and—and everything, it's not what you think.'

'Could you be more specific?'

'Sorry?'

'Would you care to explain what it is I'm thinking?'

Roxanne gazed at him, flustered by memories of what he had overheard and by his unexpected presence.

'Er. . .I realise how it must look, me saying goodbye dressed like——'

As she glanced down at her wrap and the white lace nightdress it covered, her embarrassment grew. She had considered herself to be respectable, but now the satin seemed to cling, turning each curve into a provocation, and the V where the creamy swell of her breasts was exposed had become only an inch away from indecent.

'Dressed like what?' Guy prompted as she pulled the wrap closer around her. He stretched out a hand to touch a dark curl which lay on her shoulder. 'Looking delightfully tumbled?'

Roxanne stepped back. 'I'm not.'

Her prim withdrawal amused him and his lips twitched into a smile. 'How about damn near naked?'

'That's not true!'

'Those two thin layers don't leave much to the imagination,' Guy said, laughing at such a heated denial. 'Relax, Rox. You're too uptight. As keen as you are to earn your *own* money, I doubt you'd go so far as to acquire it from the horizontal position.' He paused, his eyes full of mischief. 'Though it would be interesting to hear more about this relief which you provide.'

Roxanne frowned down at her feet. He had spoken the truth. She was too uptight, too intense, far too conscious of Guy as male and herself as female. Yet in speaking like this and touching her hair he did not mean anything; he was simply a young man playing a game. She took a breath. She would play games, too.

'Hear?' she queried, smiling at him from

beneath her lashes. 'Wouldn't it be better if I showed you?'

His mouth twitched again. 'Much.'

'Then, please, come in.'

In the two weeks since her futile attempt at persuasion, Roxanne had convinced herself—more or less—that there was nothing to be gained from talking to Guy Slaney a second time. She had even rung Karen and informed her it was no go. But now his arrival inspired a change of mind. He would not have come to announce an about-turn on *Assignment Paris*, that much was certain, yet, whatever the reason, fate had brought him to her door. Who was she to thumb her nose at fate? Or to waste an opportunity? She slid him a glance. Previously he had been deep in the throes of jet lag, but now he was wide-awake—and, surely, more inclined to be reasonable, flexible, *persuaded*?

'Welcome,' she grinned as he strode into the hall.

Guy gazed around at the white walls, the cream carpet, the leafy plants reflected in a huge oval mirror. 'So,' he said, 'you're living in luxury with a bloke who looks like every woman's dream of a sultry Arab sheik.'

'Oh, I'm not living with him. Salim is——' Roxanne began, but was hustled onwards.

'He spent the night here, didn't he?'

'Yes, but——'

'He comes to see you from time to time?'

'He comes to *stay* from time to time,' she said, unsettled by the abrupt shift in his mood. Moments ago Guy had found her hot-faced embarrassment entertaining, now he was stern and critical. Presumably the visible evidence of her supposed affluence offended him? 'However, we don't——'

'Sleep together?'

'Of course not! Salim's staying at the flat while he learns English, that's all,' Roxanne said, determined that, come what may, this time she would develop the point. 'He's been attending college for six weeks already, and has another two weeks to go.'

Guy's displeasure eased, though only by a notch. 'How much do you charge him?' he demanded.

'I don't. He's a family friend.'

'The desert hawk's receiving eight weeks' board and lodging free, gratis and for nothing? You do realise you've missed out on a good opportunity to earn your *own* money?'

'Not too smart, am I?' she shot back, irked by yet another side-swipe at her imagined avarice.

Guy stepped forward, placing a hand on the wall above her head and leaning over her. 'Smart or not, you're a class act, Rox. You could make a mint as a courtesan.'

'Thanks for the advice. If I ever decide to take it, I'll let you know!' she snapped, acutely aware of being trapped by the length of his body. His

nearness was disturbing. All it needed was for
her to sway a little, and she would sway into
him.

He moved closer—much to her consternation—and his manner changed again. As
amusement had given way to disapproval, so
disapproval had become. . .seduction? Whatever, that French urbanity had strolled to the
forefront. 'I can provide more than advice,' he
said softly. 'If you wish, I could give you some
practice.'

Roxanne looked up at him. When he had
kissed her before there had been a strange liquid
calm in his eyes which, she now realised, had
been a notice of intention. That calm had
returned, holding her in thrall, and anticipation
filled the air like the smell of gunpowder.

'Practice?' she echoed, and heard herself
croak.

Taking her chin in his fingers, Guy slowly
bent his head. 'Like this,' he murmured, and his
mouth met hers.

For a moment, Roxanne hesitated—should
she allow him to kiss her, yes or no? Common
sense plumped for no, but went ignored, for his
mouth was working a strange magic. As he
coaxed her lips apart, she blossomed like a dry
plant watered. It seemed like a lifetime since she
had last been kissed *properly*, and, unlike his
previous one, this kiss was firm and thorough
and surprisingly serious.

'Your hair smells of apples,' Guy murmured, momentarily deserting her mouth to bury his face in the mass of shiny raven-dark curls. 'Sun-ripened apples. Sweet and tangy.'

He kissed her a second time, and as his tongue stroked hers a warmth suffused the depths of her body. The hunger she had dammed up for so long spilled over, closing her mind and her senses to everything but the feel of his mouth on hers, the nearness of him. Lost in emotion, Roxanne wrapped her arms around his neck. Her breasts had tightened, her skin felt tender to the touch, and now contact was what she wanted. Contact was what she needed. Contact was what she craved. Crushing her breasts against the hard muscles of his chest, she revelled in his strength, his power, his *maleness*. Closer and closer she clung, until the pressure of his thighs on hers irredeemably revealed the effect she was having on him.

'Oh,' she said, drawing back.

Guy gave a rueful grin of self-derision. 'What did you expect?'

Embarrassment scorched her skin. Roxanne had never expected the two of them to become locked in an embrace— nor that she would react so positively. As a young widow she had attracted a number of advances, yet all had been firmly repelled. Why hadn't she repelled him? What made Guy Slaney any different?

'About *Assignment Paris*,' she said, at a rush.

Now that it had fled, her desire had become alarming. When she thought of the wanton way she had pressed herself against him, she wanted to disappear into a hole in the ground. A deep one. 'Look at the series from a——'

'We're back to that *again*?' He flung her a scurrilous look. 'When the good Lord was dishing out paranoia, you must have stood in line twice—if not three times!'

Roxanne ignored him. 'Look at the series realistically and you'll see that the repeats are of no great consequence, but the important thing to consider is the principle involved if you kill them dead.'

'Principle?'

She nodded vigorously. 'If you intend to recompense some people, then you're admitting to qualms over your use of the contract veto. But it stands to reason that those qualms can't be selective, they cover the entire cast. Which means,' she announced, with more than a tinge of triumph, 'that morally you must recognise the need to recompense everyone. However, obviously that'd be too expensive, so——'

'This is why you engineered our clinch—to persuade me to agree to the damned repeats?' Guy demanded.

Roxanne stared. She had imagined he would consider the argument she had so carefully constructed and accept its validity—not accuse her of below-the-belt manipulation.

'I didn't engineer anything!' she protested. 'You kissed me!'

'You sure as hell responded. However, I'm sorry to disappoint, but if I'm to be persuaded you'll need to put more up front than a couple of kisses.' His eyes skated to the open door of her room where the bed lay in crumpled disarray. 'Much more.'

In alarm, her gaze followed his. Was Guy playing games again. . .or making a serious suggestion? Was he prepared to bargain that way? Did he think *she* would be?

'Out of the question!' Roxanne said, just to be on the safe side.

He shrugged. 'Pity. Those sessions of make-believe love for the camera made me everlastingly curious about what it'd be like for real. Still,' he continued, his look going to where the jut of her nipples lifted the fine satin, 'at least now I know you're not frigid.'

His eyes were bold and unrelenting; beneath them the tips of her breasts seemed to *prickle*. So much so that Roxanne had to fight the urge to cross her hands over her chest.

'Whatever made you think I was?' she asked, and walked quickly away through the arch which opened on to the living-room.

Guy strolled in after her. 'We were supposed to be lovers, yet although you acted you never once *reacted*,' he said, dropping down on to the sofa. 'Not on a personal level.'

'I wasn't aware I was meant to,' she retorted.

'You weren't, but I never saw a glimmer of recognition that I existed on any other level than neutral.'

'You would have preferred me to go gaga?' Roxanne demanded, wishing she could relegate him to a neutral level now. But with his long legs stretched out in his close-fitting jeans he looked formidably masculine.

'No. I just—— There was I,' he said, losing his patience, 'swashbuckling around as *zee gendarme* who was supposed to turn women—all women—to potters' clay. And there were you, the one who received my attentions first-hand, treating me like a eunuch!'

Her brow furrowed. She knew she had been distracted—with calamities coming at her from all sides, her focus had, of necessity, been elsewhere—but had she been so aloof? If so, it had been unintentional.

'You think I spoiled your performance?' Roxanne asked.

'There was no performance to spoil,' Guy came back at her savagely. 'I'm ashamed to say I hammed my way through. No, what I found so infuriating was being treated as if I were damn near invisible. Mind you, now I wish I had been,' he muttered. 'I only needed five minutes on the set to know there was no hope of rescuing the unbelievable script—not with

that director. He'd have been incapable of direct-
ing musical chairs!'

'But why take the part if you already had
doubts about it?'

'Panic,' came the succinct reply. 'After a busy
period, my career had suddenly stalled. I knew
acting was a greasy pole, but at the time I wasn't
mature enough to keep my cool and hang on
until something decent came along. I should
have found myself a job outside the profession
and marked time, instead of which when I heard
they were casting for *Assignment Paris* I decided
anything would be better than nothing. But the
sensible thing would've been to opt out on day
one.'

'Why didn't you?' Roxanne enquired.

'Because my departure would've messed up
too many things for too many people,' he told
her. 'For instance, it was your first acting job,
and a starring one at that—though you didn't
seem impressed.'

'I wasn't,' she agreed, perching herself on the
arm of a chair. 'The media made a big thing out
of how the director had seen my picture on a
magazine cover and signed me up, but——' She
pulled a face.

'You suspected he'd done it as a way of
getting free publicity, plus a leading lady on the
cheap?' Guy suggested.

Roxanne laughed. 'No, though you're probably right.'

'So, if you weren't keen either, why did you take your role?'

She looked down at her hands. 'I needed the money.'

'Needed?' he questioned, and a sliver of steel entered his voice. 'Come off it, Rox. You were a much-sought-after model. You must have been raking it in.'

'I was, but. . .my father took ill and caring for his needs came expensive. Why are you here?' she enquired, performing a swift veer. Start talking about her personal life and she entered a dodgy area, one she preferred to avoid.

'To ask if I could take Barney to see Emma again. I've visited the old harridan twice since we last met, and each time she's looked past me and demanded to know why I haven't brought her little darling. It'd do wonders for my status if I could produce him,' he said drolly.

'Go ahead.'

'So straightforward?' Guy fixed her with cool brown eyes. 'You don't intend to trade him off against *Assignment Paris*?'

Roxanne shook her head. 'When did you want to make the visit?'

'I thought around two o'clock this afternoon?'

'That's fine.'

'It seems very quiet,' he remarked. 'How so? Is Barney out now?'

'Out like a light. He's in bed, catching up on

his sleep after being awake—and keeping me awake—half the night.'

'He's not ill, though?'

'Barnaby is in the rudest of health,' she replied pungently. 'However, for some reason or other, he's become obsessed with making raspberry noises—so at three a.m. there he was, merrily blasting forth! It took me ages to get him back to sleep.'

Guy gave a rueful smile. 'I'm sorry.'

'You're sorry?' Roxanne shot him a look. 'You mean *you* taught him how to blow raspberries?'

'It took his mind off chucking the groceries out of the pushchair.'

'Maybe, but if you teach him anything in future I'd be grateful if you could make it something quieter—like chess!'

He laughed, then looked about him. Painted ivory, the pale-carpeted living-room had white, aquamarine and lime-green flowered curtains, with the colours repeated in unusually shaped pieces of glass displayed on the mantelpiece and in the arched alcoves on either side. The contrast of light and vivid added zest to a room which, with only a white leather sofa and chairs, maple sideboard and matching drinks cabinet, was simply furnished.

'Whoever suggested your colour scheme, I like it,' he said. 'I like the lack of clutter, too. There are clean lines here, and style. It's a room to feel comfortable in.'

'Thanks.'

Guy rose to inspect twin water-colour sea-scapes which hung between the leaded-light windows. 'I look forward to the day when my place is something like this,' he said, turning to face her, 'though I doubt it ever will.'

'Your house could be lovely,' Roxanne protested.

'At a price, but I'm not in your husband's financial league, so whichever design consultant he employed I could never afford them. Alas,' Guy said, becoming jokey, 'those who have the know-how to produce perfection like this are out of the reach of a poor actor.'

A small seed planted itself in her brain and she stood up. 'Would the poor actor care to take a look through the rest of the flat?' she enquired.

'Somebody's had some excellent ideas here,' Guy praised, as she showed him through the cottage-style kitchen with its pine-tabled dining area, the spare bedroom where one wall was pinned with straw hats, the sophisticated steel-grey and white bathroom, and back into the hall.

'They're low-cost ideas. The water-colours you were admiring cost a tenner at Portobello Road market. The old typewriter I use as a plant holder came from a jumble sale. And,' she pointed to the bench beside the telephone, 'that's a Victorian church pew which was salvaged from scrap.'

Guy ran appreciative fingertips over the carved, honey-coloured wood. 'Whoever's responsible has flair.'

Roxanne grinned. 'And you'd like them to work for you?'

'I'd be bloody delighted!'

'Then let me.'

'You?' He stared. 'You mean you——?'

She nodded. 'I chose the colours, painted the rooms, made the curtains and cushions, found the smaller items of the furniture. Shortly after my marriage I did a course in interior design,' she explained.

'And you learned how to do a place up like this?'

'The course taught me the basics, and a collection of good do-it-yourself books provided the rest. It's amazing what can be achieved if you try. The flat was dull when we moved in—most of the light had been soaked up by a sludge green carpet and the paintwork was faded—but it had possibilities. So does your house. Give me the opportunity and I'll——'

Guy cut her dead. 'This is your new game plan?' he demanded.

'I beg your pardon?'

'I assume that while you've accepted I won't be agreeing to the repeats—at long last!—you reckon I still owe you, and, surprise, surprise, this interior decorating is going to cost me near enough the sum you would have received from a second run of *Assignment Paris*? It might be amazing what can be achieved by trying,' he said tersely, 'but no, thanks. I don't con that easily.'

'I'm not conning you! I decorated the flat on the cheap and I'll do the same for you,' Roxanne protested. 'All you'll pay for are the materials and any work I'm unable to do myself—like resiting light-switches, or connecting up a washer, or tiling a shower. However, I know a team of reliable plumbers and electricians who charge very reasonable prices.'

'You'd be working for free?' Guy demanded, his eyes tight with suspicion.

'Yes. On one condition. Well, two, really.'

He snorted. 'I knew there'd be a catch.'

'I'd like you to give two parties and invite around forty people—all of whom live in their own homes and who can afford to use an interior decorator. The same guests to come on both occasions.'

'That's the most interesting idea I've heard in years!' he said facetiously.

'One to take place with your house in its present condition,' she continued, 'and the other after I've completed the transformation.' Roxanne tilted her head. 'I assume you don't like giving parties?'

'You have a great way with understatment. I'm happy to ask a few pals in for a drink, but to provide hospitality for forty!' His expression was unadulterated horror.

'Thirty will do.'

'Big deal. And the idea, I suppose, is that when everyone sees the improvements they'll be so overcome with admiration that they'll clamour to give you commissions?'

'With luck. If you don't have sufficient friends who fall into the right category, ask colleagues, acquaintances. You must know a lot of people,' she coaxed.

Guy sighed, and began to mull over her proposition. 'I'm the key to your future?' he enquired.

'You could be.'

Roxanne's agreement was reluctant. She did not want to pass over control of her life to anyone, in any way, ever again. Yet, in this instance, she needed Guy Slaney.

'You're this serious about earning your *own* money?' he demanded.

'I am.'

She was in deadly earnest. Although it was essential that she relaunch herself into some kind of career, the aim had been to wait until Barnaby was older, but the huge advantage of interior decorating was that she could do it now, with him in tow! Why had she never thought of it before? Roxanne wondered. When she toured the shops for paint and fabrics, the little boy could go with her, and when she was busy at someone's house he could play at her feet. She gave a wry smile. The idea of Barnaby obediently playing day-in, day-out seemed overly optimistic, but surely Mrs Ashby would take him for the occasional afternoon?

'Guy, the parties won't cost you a thing in either effort or money. All you need to do is be there,' she appealed. 'I'll clean your house before and tidy it afterwards. I'll work out a buffet menu, then buy and prepare the food. Cold meats, quiches and salads? Curried fish, sweet and sour pork, and rice? Fresh fruit salad, gâteaux, and a selection of cheeses for dessert?' Roxanne said, the suggestions tumbling out in an unstoppable, breathless flow. 'I'll bring extra glasses, plates and cutlery, and wash everything up. Plus I'll organise a couple of waitresses. The porter here has two daughters who'll be happy to help. They're half Filipino, very pretty. I'll also arrange the drinks,' her face clouded, 'though not spirits. I'll get wine-boxes from the supermarket and make a fruit punch. Well,' she said, reaching the end of her spiel, 'what do you think?'

In silence he surveyed her, slowly rubbing a thumbnail across his lower lip. 'I think,' Guy said, at last, 'that you can have your initial shindig, then start work on my house. But,' he ignored the thanks already bursting from her, 'if I find I'm being overcharged for as much as one pot of paint, then you, lady, are out!'

CHAPTER FOUR

AS REHEARSALS for his play were due to begin in ten days' time, the first soirée would be held the weekend before—so Guy decreed.

'But that's much too short notice,' Roxanne had wailed. 'You can't spring a night out on people and take it for granted they'll be free. They need more warning.'

Her protests received short shrift. He was adamant. If she wanted the event to take place in the foreseeable future, then next Saturday it must be. Given no alternative, she had agreed, only to then fret over whether the unwilling host might drag his feet and fail to invite the requisite numbers. It was not so. Having committed himself, Guy put his doubts about the party—and her—to one side, and entered into the spirit of things. A guest list was compiled and a multitude of phone calls made. On the spur of the moment he had decided on a gathering, would so-and-so care to attend? So-and-so would. Please. Please. Please. The spate of acceptances delighted and amazed her. Either Guy must be ultra-popular, or his invitation had been embellished with promises of fireworks, unlimited champagne, and star-spangled dancing girls.

'What's the final count?' Roxanne enquired, following him into the kitchen on the ordained evening. It was an hour before the masses were due to arrive and, after preparing the bulk of the food at home, she had just shipped everything over in a taxi. She set down an earthenware casserole. 'Any last-minute cancellations?'

'None,' Guy replied as he made a place on the work-surface for the basket of crusty rolls which comprised his final load. 'There are still thirty-eight definites, and two who can't be certain but who intend to move heaven and earth to get here. Don't panic,' he said drily, 'if they don't turn up there's bound to be some bright spark who arrives dragging an extra body or two behind them.'

'If the head-count goes over, that's fine,' she grinned. 'I've catered on the generous side, so the food'll stretch.' Roxanne took a swatch of materials from one of the carrier-bags which were dotted around. 'How about this for the cloakroom? You remember we agreed to do away with curtains and hang a blind instead? I thought the crimson and white onion pattern might be good.'

'I'm to look at *more* samples?' he protested.

Over the past week, Roxanne had been busy—both with arrangements for the party and making tentative refurbishment plans. A morning had been spent pacing the Chelsea house and, after taking copious measurements and notes, she had gone away for a long, hard think. The next day she had approached Guy with a variety of suggestions and ideas. And later, when most of these had been agreed and a budget fixed, she had sallied forth to scrutinise the do-it-yourself stores and fabric shops. Already colour schemes had been roughed out for the upper storey and now she was eager to start on the ground floor.

'If you have a moment,' she smiled.

'I have several, but aren't there things you should be doing?' Guy asked, gazing around at what seemed to be the contents of a fair-sized delicatessen.

She shook her head. 'Everything's organised. Suzi and Kim are due in fifteen minutes, and as soon as they arrive we'll get to work.'

'I'm surprised you're not wearing something more appropriate,' he said when the material had received his approval.

Roxanne looked down at her navy and white striped top and beige trousers. 'Like what?'

'As you've been so correct in every other area—fresh flowers all over the place, napkins matching the table cover et cetera—shouldn't you be clad in official waitress uniform? Lace cap, tight white bodice and a saucy black skirt revealing yards and yards of shapely fish-netted leg,' Guy elucidated.

'I intended to,' she replied, deadpan, 'until I

remembered that I shall be stationed exclusively in the kitchen.'

'Curses!' His despair was of the anguished sigh variety. 'So I'll need to seek solace in my rich fantasy life?'

"Fraid so.'

After a week of being in his company almost daily, Roxanne was becoming skilled at playing his games. It had been a long time since her repartee had been tested in such a way, but she was a fast learner, and teasing and joking with him was fun.

'As the perfect host you ought to be decked out in white tie and tails,' she told him, in sassy dismissal of his peat-brown shirt and tailored trousers, 'but I'll settle for you just being the perfect host. Don't bother about what's going on back here; that's my job. Yours is to welcome the guests and keep them happy.'

'I love it when you get bossy,' Guy said, with a grinning shudder of delight. 'Ever thought of buying a whip?'

'And please don't tell anyone what the party's in aid of,' Roxanne continued. 'If they're left to discover the transformation for themselves, the impact will be all the greater.'

'I'm not allowed to draw their attention to my abode's current resemblance to a flophouse?'

'You may make a subtle reference—and invite them to take a tour—but don't give the game away.'

'My lips are sealed.'

'Not too sealed to blow up a few balloons?'
she asked, passing over a selection in red, white
and blue. 'If you fasten them to the front gate,
everyone'll know where to come.'

'The girl thinks of *everything*. These wouldn't
last long if Barney was around,' Guy remarked,
between puffs.

'No, and he didn't last long when you brought
him home, either. He managed to keep his eyes
open long enough to eat something, then it was
into bed and fast asleep. Now Salim's guaranteed undisturbed baby-sitting. It was good of
you to take Barney out this afternoon.' Roxanne
smiled as she lined up salad stuffs. 'It allowed
me to do everything in half the time.'

'Barney?' Guy enquired.

'If you can't beat 'em, join 'em,' she said in
wry resignation, and he laughed. 'Barney had a
whale of a time today. You obviously have a
knack with kids.'

'At the last count my four sisters had supplied
me with a couple of nieces or nephews apiece,
so I've put in plenty of practice.'

Roxanne looked up from the tomatoes she
was slicing. 'You have four sisters?'

'I do. The Press haven't discovered them yet
and, if it's up to me, they never will. Reporters
are always wanting to know about my private
life, but——' he pulled down his mouth '—I
never talk about it.'

'Why not?'

'Two reasons. Firstly, because there are more people involved than just me. And, secondly, because I'm damned if I'm going to fall into the trap of believing I'm of interest merely because I happen to be an actor.'

As Guy knotted the first balloon and picked up a second, Roxanne became pensive. How different everything would have been—would be—if Hamish had had a similar attitude but, in addition to loving the limelight, he had believed the Press were there to be *used*, and that anyone who did not take advantage was a fool. So he had agreed to be interviewed by anyone who'd asked, and had sometimes sought meetings himself. She sighed. Regrettably, the information her husband had passed on to the reporters had often owed more to fable than fact.

Two and a half hours later, the party was in full swing and, judging from the hum of conversation and laughter beyond the kitchen door, the guests were having a happy time. At intervals her sloe-eyed helpers came in to replenish the punch bowl or deposit used glasses, and then Roxanne would catch a glimpse of a face and a few garbled words. Some people she recognised as celebrities, some she did not. However, among the guests was a svelte blonde whom she had been introduced to on the set of *Assign-ment Paris*—Prue Graham.

The first to arrive, she and her host had, according to Suzi's giggled report, gone into a doorstep clinch which had lasted minutes.

'Guy, my darling!' Roxanne had heard the actress cry, her clear voice carrying. 'I never thought *you'd* host a party.'

'Neither did I,' he had muttered, then the door had closed and subsequent dialogue had been lost.

Could Guy and Prue still be close? she wondered, as she went back and forth between kitchen and dining-room putting finishing touches to the buffet table. He had made no mention of the actress, or any other woman come to that, yet he *had* invited her this evening, she *had* arrived with astonishing eagerness, and there *had* been a clinch. On her tour of the house Roxanne had seen no sign of female occupancy, so if Guy and Prue were having an affair it did not include them living together. Yet cohabitation was not the be-all and end-all. Some couples preferred space. Even husbands and wives were known to live apart these days. Roxanne frowned as she checked the frequency of the serving spoons. If Guy was in the middle of a romance it made no difference to her—none at all—but. . .Karen was the authority on show-biz couplings, perhaps she should phone and ask for the low-down?

'Coping OK?' Guy enquired, walking into the kitchen a short time later.

She nodded. 'The cold dishes are set out in the dining-room, and the hot ones are waiting in the oven.' She gestured towards the babble of sound. 'How's it going?'

He stole a peach slice from one of the bowls of fruit salad and, head tipped back, slid it into his mouth. 'To be honest, better than I expected.'

'You can't be having a good time?' Roxanne grinned.

'Sort of.'

'Is everybody here?'

'All present and correct,' he reported, licking juice from his fingers. 'Except one who's sent a message to say he'll be arriving later. Much later.'

'Then we should start the meal?'

Guy purloined another slice of peach. 'Please do. Being the perfect host is hungry work. I'm starving.'

If the host was famished, so, it appeared, were the guests. Suzi and Kim sped in from the dining-room with reports of people loading their plates, then returning for second helpings, and third. And when desserts were served, these were wolfed back with as much fervour as the main course. The cheeseboard was offered, and coffee. Finally liqueurs, which Guy had financed, went the rounds. At intervals throughout the meal her assistants had been traipsing in with dirty plates, bowls and cutlery, and Roxanne had managed to keep pace—but now a mountain of washing-up built up around her. Filling the sink with yet more warm, soapy water, she had just begun on another load when the door swung open. Slim and elegant in a white, Grecian-style silk dress, Prue Graham strolled in.

'I realise the kitchen is normally out of bounds, but I felt I must sneak through to say thanks to the person responsible for such a delicious meal,' she enthused, but half-way across the linoleum her golden-sandalled foot faltered and she came to a full stop. 'Oh, it's you.'

One moment graciously smiling, the actress's mouth now pinched to a lipsticked slash and hostility shone from her blue eyes. Roxanne looked at her in confusion. Why the change? What had she ever done to her? Their single meeting had been brief, and four years ago. Then a painful void opened up in her heart. Like Guy, Prue must believe she had married for money—and despised her for it. Perhaps the blonde had been one of the critics whom Guy had defended her against?

'I'm pleased you enjoyed everything,' she said quietly.

Prue stared stonily back. 'Do you live here?'

she demanded, the question emerging abrupt and brusque.

'Me?' Roxanne could not help laughing out loud. A short time ago she had been musing over the possibility of the actress's involvement with Guy, and here the actress was, wondering about *her*. 'Good grief, no!'

'Not exactly the house beautiful, is it?' Prue remarked, wrinkling her nose at the ill-lit kitchen with its meagre fittings. 'Guy's been showing people around, but, although a man might be prepared to put up with a place like this, a woman never would. You've gone into catering?' she carried on, her manner becoming friendlier. 'A wise move. People will always eat. What do you do, run your own company? My hairdresser's daughter is in your line,' she said, not waiting for an answer. 'Poppy started by hawking sandwiches around offices, but now she'd tackle a bunfight in the Albert Hall, if asked. Not that Poppy's in your league, I hasten to add. Nowhere near. It's obvious you're on the up and up. I don't do much at-home entertaining myself—not on this scale—but do you have an address card handy? Not with you,' she decided, when dripping hands were raised from the washing-up bowl in an indeterminate gesture. 'Never mind, Guy can give me the details. I suppose you realise he's on the up and up, too?' Prue enquired.

Startled to find a break in the high-speed

monologue, Roxanne cleared her throat—but got no further.

'Guy's done some memorable work in Chekhov, Shaw, Shakespeare,' the blonde declared as Kim arrived to offload yet another tray of soiled dishes. 'He's provoked intense interest with his contemporary performances, too. Everyone in the industry regards him as among the élite of actors.'

Roxanne's eyes opened wide. 'They do?'

Although Karen had described Guy's prowess in glowing terms, Roxanne had taken everything with a large pinch of scepticism. Her own foray into acting had had the journalists scribbling toe-curling phrases—as well as being 'a sultry beauty of uncanny ability', she had even been described as the next Garbo, and if that wasn't proof that they exaggerated beyond belief, what was? Yet if the people Guy worked among considered him to be special, then the compliments he had garnered must be based on something more solid than froth.

'Why do you imagine so many of his guests cancelled previous engagements in order to be here tonight?' Prue demanded. 'It's because they want to be able to boast to their grandchildren that the great Guy Slaney once invited them to his home.'

The *great* Guy Slaney? The actress was spreading it thick. . .and yet everyone *had* accepted his invitation.

'But he wanders around Chelsea in a pair of worn jeans,' Roxanne protested. 'I mean, he's ——' She stopped. The word on the tip of her tongue had been 'ordinary', and Guy was anything but that.

The blonde laughed. 'Don't be fooled by his back-street cred. It's typical of Guy that he should buck the system.' Her expression became serious. 'Yet continued success in acting is a fragile thing—it depends on natural aptitude, luck, and an instinct for making the right choices. Still, Guy's got his head screwed on.'

'Do you remember the series he and I did together?' Roxanne enquired hesitantly. 'It wasn't too clever. Do you think a repeat could——'

'A repeat?' Peals of laughter rang out. 'With all due respect, no one in their right mind would ever repeat that! And thank goodness, because it was the one error Guy's made in an otherwise faultless body of work. If an actor wants the ultimate stamp of approval, he must appear on the West End stage,' Prue pronounced, changing course, 'which is what he'll be doing in another month or so. He's never been one to follow the easy route, but agreeing to play that particular part takes courage. He'll be on stage every minute, and the success of the entire production rests on his shoulders. If he pulls it off, and I'm sure he will, it'll be a *tour de force*. Tickets are being snapped up already. Everybody who's anybody intends to be there.

Thanks again for the feast.' The blonde smiled, and wafted across to the door. 'Bye.'

Left alone, Roxanne continued the washing-up. She had had no idea Guy was scaling such dizzy heights, and she was most impressed. But the higher you climbed, the greater the danger of falling—and the further you fell. Her brow furrowed. She had attributed his stubbornness over *Assignment Paris* to ego and nit-picking pride, but Prue's comment on the fragility of success suggested otherwise. Had her judgement been too hasty, too ill-informed, too harsh? she wondered. If he was involved in self-preservation—and now it seemed possible—that was something she understood.

'Anything left to eat?' Guy enquired, waltzing in around Kim who had completed another laden journey.

'You can't still be hungry!' Roxanne protested.

'I'm not. But the late arrival's just put in an appearance, plus a hanger-on. Chris says not to bother, but the bloke he's brought has obviously drunk far too much of the falling-down water, and I'd feel happier if he ate something before he *does* fall down.'

'No problem. I kept some food aside specially.'

The latercomers were served, the washing-up completed, her crockery repacked in an assortment of boxes and bags. At one o'clock the first guests began to drift away. Although tardy

departure was the hallmark of any successful
party, and Roxanne was relieved it had gone so
well, now she longed for everyone to leave. It
had been a busy day, and she was weary. On
hearing further farewells, she thanked her two
assistants, paid them their wages, and sent them
home in a taxi. All that remained was for her to
wash the glasses belonging to the dilatory clus-
ter of guests, and empty the ashtrays. Tomorrow she would return and set the house
properly to rights.

More goodbyes sounded. More cars drove
away. Opening the fridge, Roxanne checked the
remnants of the buffet which she had wrapped
in cling film. That piece of cheese could be used
in an omelette for her and Barnaby, and the little
boy would enjoy the helping of fruit salad, too.
As for the remaining gâteau, perhaps Guy——

Footsteps thudded behind her, swarthy arms
encircled her waist, and, without warning, she
was grabbed back against a substantial, pot-
bellied figure.

'Hey!' Roxanne protested, in breathless alarm.

'I've had my eye on you, my oriental beauty,
ever since I arrived,' a voice cackled into her ear.
'Don't think you can escape. Mine host has
taken my pal into his study to show him some
old book or other, which leaves you and me
here—all alone!'

In danger of being asphyxiated by whisky

fumes, Roxanne grabbed at the podgy hands which held her.

'I think,' she snapped, wrenching them smartly apart, 'you have made a mistake!'

Ready to deliver a sharp-edged rebuke, she swivelled, and as she did her protest died. The mauler was Athol Wallace—alcoholic, scrounger *extraordinaire*, and Hamish's one-time business partner. How did he come to be at the party? she wondered in bewilderment. He could not possibly know Guy—could he? Then it registered that he must be the tipsy character who had accompanied the late arrival.

'Roxie!' the balding Scot blubbered in surprise, and, staggering backwards, he plonked his bulky form down on a chair—thought more by good luck than good management. 'Long time no see. I never thought I'd come across you again.'

'Guy Slaney is. . .a neighbour, and I'm helping him with the catering,' Roxanne said quickly. Her eyes darkened to a stormy grey. 'I assume you've latched on to some unsuspecting friend of his and invited yourself along for free food and drink—as usual?'

'Now, Roxie, don't be nasty,' he appealed. 'I'm a friend of the family.'

'You're no friend of mine!'

'I was Hamish's friend. Me an' Hamish were pals. Great pals. Me an' Hamish went back a long way, to when he was married to Janet.

Lovely girl, Janet,' he crooned, slurring the words. 'Lovely, lovely girl. Long black hair and great figure, just like you. Pity she had to go and die. Pity old Hamish had to go and smash himself to smithereens. Pity he had to leave you and the bairn skint.'

Roxanne closed the fridge door. 'I beg your pardon?' she said carefully.

'Skint, busted, down to your last shilling,' Athol expounded, his basso profundo voice rolling around. 'Y'know what I mean.'

Her mouth tightened. 'I haven't the slightest idea.'

'Roxie, Roxie,' he chided, 'you don't need to pretend with me.' Ready for a pow-wow, he shifted to the edge of his chair. 'We both understand how Hamish didn't want it to be spread abroad that all his lovely money had run out, and it won't. Mum's the word.' He fumbled a salute. 'Scout's honour. But we bumped into each other in a bar one night, and he got a wee bit drunk, and—well, he confessed all.'

Roxanne stared at him in alarm. Was he telling the truth? Could Hamish have confided in this associate from his youth? It had been rare that he drank, but when he had it had made him talkative. Had he been *too* talkative? Long ago she had accepted that Mr Hussein knew about some of her husband's losses, though not all, but had Athol been let in on the secret, too? A shiver settled near her heart.

'It's you who were drunk,' she retorted. 'And you're drunk now!'

Athol dragged a handkerchief from his pocket and mopped beads of sweat from his bright red face. 'Reminded me of the head of a diplomatic corps, did Hamish. Always so beautifully turned out. Looked like a success, yet hated to be associated with failure. But he did love a gamble, and towards the end there weren't enough bums on the seats at those shows of his, were there? Poor Hamish.' He sat for a minute, morosely shaking his head. 'So, what have you been doin' with yourself, Roxie?' he enquired. 'Got yourself a new man?'

'No.'

He clambered to his feet. 'Want one?'

'No, thanks.'

'It's two years since poor Hamish kicked it, and you can't tell me you're happy sleeping alone. Not a sexy wee lass like you.' Athol reeled towards her. 'Like someone to cuddle up to? An older man?'

At his approach, Roxanne stepped back so hard against the fridge that her elbows almost pierced the door. The Scot may have entered the kitchen in chase of Suzi or Kim, but in the past his lewd winks and oh, so casual touches had made his desire for her plain. Only her husband's presence had held him in check, but her husband had gone, and now he was bearing down.

'Keep away from me,' she warned.

'I thought you liked older men. You liked Hamish.' He placed beefy hands on either side of her head and leaned down, trapping her. 'There's no reason why you couldn't like me.'

'There are hundreds!' Roxanne declared, turning her head aside to escape the blast of unsavoury fumes. If he breathed into her face again, she would throw up.

'You could like me if you tried,' Athol wheedled.

'Would you kindly stand aside?' she demanded.

'No.'

'Let me go!' she flared, and pushed hard against his chest.

Earlier his hold had been easily broken, but now her admirer was prepared and more determined. When her first push proved ineffective she tried to heave him away again, but he was as solid and immovable as a tank.

'Be nice to me, Roxie, and I'll be nice to you,' he muttered, and, pitching forward, he pressed thick, wet lips to her cheek.

Roxanne's skin crawled. She had to get away, so what should she do—slap his fat face, or stamp on his foot, or give a blood-curdling yell? She lifted her hand—but Athol grabbed hold. She ground down her foot—but he sidestepped. She made to shout—and he clamped a sweaty paw over her mouth. Roxanne almost gagged. Inebriated he might be, yet her assailant possessed disturbing cunning and strength. But she had to escape that clammy muzzle of a hand. She must breathe in air. Now! Panic erupted. This way and that she squirmed, struggling for release, until suddenly, as if by magic, her assailant was lifted from her.

Mouth agape and bloodshot eyes astonished, Athol was propelled across the room and pinioned against a wall. A thud sounded as his head jolted back.

'What the hell do you think you're doing?' his host snarled, looming over him.

'Er—nothing.'

'Did he hurt you?' Guy barked, almost incandescent with fury.

Roxanne gasped in a breath. 'No.'

'You're sure?' he demanded, as though she need demonstrate only minuscule doubt and the Scot would be rapidly torn limb from limb.

'I'm sure.'

'Her husband and I were buddies, and we were talking about the old times.' Athol peered pleadingly out from behind Guy's shoulder. 'Tell him, Roxie. Tell him about me and Hamish. Did you know Roxie's husband?' he asked Guy when she remained mute.

'No.'

'But you'd seen him around?'

'From time to time. Look, you son of a bitch, I don't give a damn who you are,' he growled. 'In future you keep well away from Roxanne, and you stay clear of my house. Understand?'

'Yes, sir. Will do. Wonderful man, Hamish,' Athol muttered, wandering off down memory lane. 'Best pal in the world. Pity about——'

'He's drunk,' Roxanne said quickly.

'Very,' Guy agreed.

'And talking rubbish,' she added, as insurance against the Scot also wandering into an indiscretion.

Abruptly the kitchen door was opened and a bearded young man looked in. 'Where is everyone?' he asked, then, summing up the situation, he grimaced. 'Having trouble? Sorry.'

'Chris, you brought this individual and I'd be grateful if you'd remove him,' Guy rasped. 'Soonest!'

'I never intended him to come along,' the newcomer apologised as Athol's lids took a decisive droop. 'I don't know him that well. But I met him in the street and foolishly let it slip that I was going to a party, and from then on the old bastard stuck to me like glue. Time to leave,' he informed his charge. 'Say goodnight.'

'G'night,' Athol mumbled.

As the two men helped him out through the house and into a car, Roxanne followed. The Scot appeared to have begun sleepwalking now, but she needed to be on her guard. He had said she could trust him to keep quiet about Hamish and, as she had neither heard rumours nor been approached by the Press, it seemed that for two years he *had* been discreet. But seeing her had revived memories, and if he started blethering on about her husband again she must, somehow, shut him up. Tense and subdued, she waited, and gave a sigh of relief when Athol was driven away.

'Are you sure you're all right?' Guy queried as they went into the living-room. Frowning, he surveyed her face. 'You look very pale.'

'I'm tired, that's all,' she assured him. 'Thanks for rescuing me.' She bent to lift some glasses. 'I'll just wash these and——'

He placed a restraining hand on her arm. 'Leave them. I'll ring for a taxi and——'

'You mustn't! I've spent far too much on this evening already,' Roxanne protested, then, realising what she had said, she flushed. How ironic that she should have been in terror of Athol's indiscretions, then promptly come out with one of her own! Though Guy would imagine she was simply penny-pinching. 'I'd rather walk,' she said, with a bright smile. 'It's been hot and stuffy in the kitchen and—and I'd like to cool down.'

'But it's gone two a.m. You can't set off alone through the streets now.'

'I'll be OK.'

Guy shook his head. 'No way. Get your jacket, I'll walk you home.'

CHAPTER FIVE

THE moonlit square was as still and silent as a deserted film set. Street lamps shone golden circles, lighting the pavements, a leafy branch of a tree, the façades of the houses, but all the windows were dark. When they turned the corner, an empty street stretched out ahead. Not a soul was in sight. Walking along through the starlit night, Roxanne felt as though they were the only two people in the whole of London.

'I would have paid for your taxi,' Guy said, all of a sudden. 'In fact, I want to pay for the party. I'd be grateful if tomorrow you'd total up how much everything cost and——'

'I'm financing this evening,' she said firmly. 'It was decided.'

'Rox, when I agreed I never realised what the feeding of forty souls would involve. They must have consumed enough tonight to keep several battalions marching for a year!'

'What you agreed to was a business arrangement which still stands,' Roxanne insisted.

'But tonight you've enabled me to return all kinds of hospitality.'

'And you've enabled me to start a career.'

Guy sighed. 'You realise there's no guarantee anyone will come up with a commission?'

'I do, o ye of little faith. But, thanks to you, I now have a back-up idea. If the interior design doesn't take off, I shall go into home catering!' Roxanne announced.

He sent her a frowning sideways look. 'You really are determined to make your own money, aren't you?'

'I like to keep busy,' she replied, with a jaunty smile.

'I reckon catering could be a winner,' Guy mused as they walked on. 'Everyone kept exclaiming over the wonderful food.'

'I shall prepare a completely new menu next time,' she decided. 'Perhaps something——' Roxanne broke off to stare in horror. A small, furry alien creature had scampered from the darkness, run across only inches from their feet, and disappeared beneath a parked car. 'Guy!' she shrieked, making a wild grab for him. 'I've just seen a rat!'

He put an arm around her and smiled. 'It was a mouse.'

She shivered, went cold, felt goose-bumps rise on her skin. 'It was too big for a mouse,' she declared shakily. 'Much too big.'

'Sweetheart, it was a mouse.' Guy bent his head to look under the car. 'If we wait here for a minute you'll see——'

'Wait?' Roxanne yelped. Her hands on his arm, she dragged him hastily away. 'I'm not waiting to see a rat—or a mouse.'

'A mouse won't hurt you.'

'But rats can! I remember reading about one which ran up a man's trouser leg and——'

'Inflicted all kinds of damage?' Guy made a face. 'Sounds painful.'

'Do you think there are any more around?' she asked, her grey eyes skittering nervously from side to side.

'In any big city there must be thousands. Millions, maybe.' When she looked at him in alarm, he grinned and took hold of her hand. 'Don't worry, I'll look after you. I had a white mouse when I was a kid. Called Whitey. Very original. I took it to school once and. . .'

As he talked and made her laugh, Roxanne calmed down. After a while, she decided that if another rodent did shoot out from nowhere she would not mind—as long as Guy stayed near.

'Suppose I buy Barney a mouse?' he suggested, his mouth quirking.

'Don't bother!'

'But it's good for children to have pets.'

'Not very young children.'

'So you'll be happy for him to have a mouse when he's a bit older?'

'Yes—like twenty-five and living well away from his mother,' she replied smartly.

Guy laughed. 'Coward.'

For a few minutes they walked on in silence.

'It's funny to be holding hands,' Roxanne said, at random.

'Funny?'

'Funny nice. It seems ages since I've walked hand in hand, and it makes me feel. . .young again. And carefree.'

'You're not exactly an old lady,' he remarked with a smile.

'No, but——' she sighed '—these last few years haven't been easy. Hamish's death was traumatic enough, but it also meant that when Barnaby arrived I was virtually on my own.'

'No parents around?'

Roxanne shook her head. 'My mother died when I was nineteen and Dad around three years ago. I have a brother, but he lives abroad.'

'Then your father's expensive illness proved fatal?'

'Sorry?'

'That was the reason why you did *Assignment Paris*,' Guy reminded her.

Her heart lurched. The trouble with laundering the truth was that you needed to remember you had laundered it, and on this occasion she had forgotten.

'Oh. . .yes.'

'Was that Athol bloke telling the truth when he said he and your husband had been pals?' he enquired as they turned the corner into her street.

Roxanne's heart took another downward tip. Unpleasant though it was, her encounter with the Scot had been brief, and she had hoped it

would be short-lived in everyone's memory,
too. But her escort had asked a question, and
she must answer it.

'They weren't blood brothers or anything like
that, but twenty-five years ago they'd been
partners in a building company in Scotland, so
there was always a tie.'

'Hamish liked him?' Guy asked curiously.

'Not much. It was more that he had a weakness for lame ducks. My husband was very kind
and very generous,' Roxanne said, then
frowned as a contrary thought flickered traitor-
ously into her mind.

Guy sent her a quizzical glance through the
shadows. 'And Athol knew it and took full
advantage?' he prompted when she remained
silent.

She pushed the thought away. 'Yes.'

'What happened to the building company?'

'As long as Hamish was in charge it pros-
pered, but he moved on to bigger and better
things, and when he left——' She moved her
shoulders. 'Athol had a liking for the booze,
even then.'

'The bigger and better things were property
deals? That's how your husband made the
money which enabled him to become an
impresario?'

'Yes,' she said again.

'I seem to recall he was a millionaire before he
was thirty.'

Roxanne nodded, relieved that their arrival at the entrance to the mansion block signalled an end to what was beginning to feel like an interrogation. Removing her hand from his, she hunted for her key in her bag.

'Thanks for walking me home,' she said.

Guy grinned. 'I've not finished yet. I'm taking you to your door.'

'But——'

'From ghouls and ghosties and sozzled men and mice, I shall deliver you,' he misquoted, and accompanied her into the building and up to the third floor.

'Thanks,' she began again as they reached her door.

Guy took hold of her hand. 'Thank you,' he said, bringing it to his lips. 'I know you had a reason for pulling out all the stops tonight, but, believe me, I do appreciate everything.'

He smiled at her, and she smiled at him, and as they looked at each other Roxanne felt tiny sparks begin to shoot between them. How could Karen have said he was not good-looking? she wondered, and how could she ever have agreed? Guy was more than good-looking, he was gorgeous. She loved his tiger eyes, fringed with those thick black lashes. And the little dent in the middle of his chin—however did he manage to shave in there? And the fall of bronze hair which fell over his brow. Her fingers itched.

She wanted to touch his hair. She wanted to touch him.

'I enjoyed it,' she got out chokily.

'Apart from the last bit.' Guy's jaw hardened. 'When I saw that bastard pawing you, I felt like picking him up and throwing him straight through the damn wall!'

Roxanne grinned at his ferocity. 'You almost did.'

He nodded, his anger falling away, and kissed her hand again. 'Goodnight, sweetheart,' he murmured.

'Goodnight.'

It should have been farewell, but Guy hesitated. Was he ready to leave her? Could he tear himself away? No. Not yet. He bent and slowly, tantalisingly, trailed the tip of his tongue around the shape of her lips. Roxanne quivered. The moist tracing was so erotic, so exciting, she could barely stand still. Guy drew back to give a lopsided grin, then bent again—only this time she opened her mouth and caught the tip of his tongue between her teeth. An inch away, the gold-flecked eyes looked into hers. The world jolted. Then suddenly his arms were around her and he was kissing her with hunger, with need, almost with desperation.

'Rox,' he said huskily. '*Rox!*'

Guy plunged his hands into the raven curtain of her hair, and, wrapping it around his fingers, pulled her closer. There was no escape, though she did not want to escape. All she wanted was to feel his mouth hard on hers. To taste him. To absorb him through every pore.

When he eventually pulled away and looked at her, Roxanne gave a tremulous smile. Like hers, his breathing was erratic. Like hers must be, his eyes were glazed.

'That was—was some goodnight,' she started to say, joking in an attempt to restore a degree of normality, then suddenly she gasped.

The landing lights, which operated on a time-switch, had snapped off, plunging them into darkness.

With a low, satisfied, very masculine laugh, Guy drew her compliant body into the lean crescent of his own and began kissing her again—but, very quickly, kissing was not enough. Pushing aside her jacket, he slid his hand beneath the cotton top and began to lan-guorously stroke her midriff. Roxanne strained towards him. As much as she itched to touch him, she needed him to touch her, but she wanted more intimate caresses. Her body was crying out, pleading. His hands moved upwards, there was a moment when he released her bra, and then his fingers closed over her bare breast, trapping and gently squeezing the hard point of her nipple. A second quiver rocked through, sensitising her from shoulder to thigh. This was what she wanted. This. This. As Guy rolled the rigid peaks between a finger and thumb, Roxanne gave a low moan of pleasure. Her breasts were burning. She was burning. Flames were licking over her.

Desperately she pulled at his shirt, tugging open the buttons—then she was touching him, her hands sliding across the bronze furze of his chest, around his waist, fingering the furrow of his spine. The sensation of touching and being touched was incredible.

'Sweet mercy, Rox,' Guy groaned, his mouth hot as he buried it in her throat. 'Do you know what I feel like doing now?'

She stroked his hair. 'Picking me up and throwing me through the wall?' she murmured.

He took in a breath. 'Try again.'

'Going to bed,' she sighed, 'and so do I.'

To hear her thoughts emerge in crystalline spoken words had a dramatic effect, and Roxanne jerked back. Why had she said that? she wondered. What was she agreeing to? How could she have been so unthinking, so foolish, so carried away?

'What I mean is——' she began, hurriedly drawing down her top.

'We need to make love,' Guy completed. 'You're right. Every time we see each other there's a throb in the air, a deep attraction.'

'No, no.' Roxanne skated her hand around the wall, frantically searching for the light-switch. There was a click and the light came on, making them both blink against the glare. 'What

I meant was it's very late and—and we both need our sleep,' she gabbled, back-pedalling furiously. 'Barney'll be awake in a few hours, and if I don't grab a bit of rest I'll be useless in the morning.'

Guy pushed strands of hair back from his brow. 'Sweetheart, you want me as much as I want you,' he protested, in a driven tone.

'You're wrong! I don't want you. And—and the only reason you're interested in me is because you want to satisfy your curiosity. Sorry,' she said, summoning up an icy dignity from somewhere, 'I'm not interested in being used for investigative research.'

Guy scowled. 'You've lost me.'

'You said the sessions before the camera made you curious about——'

'I know what I damn well said!'

'Keep your voice down,' Roxanne begged. 'You'll wake everyone.'

'What did you think I had in mind?' he growled. 'A fast fumble, a eureka! now-I-know, and an even faster goodbye?'

'I've no idea, but whatever it was——'

'You're not interested in being used?' Furiously he jammed his shirt back into his trousers. 'It seems to me you've got things the wrong way around here.'

'How?'

'You, Roxanne, were at *my* house tonight. You traded on *my* goodwill. You're hoping to entice *my* friends.' Guy flung open the lift door and stepped inside. 'If there's any poor sucker being used,' he said icily, 'it's me!'

Four o'clock in the dead hours of the morning, and sleep refused to come. Going to the window, Roxanne gazed out into the night. Not very far away Guy would also be lying awake—angry with her, resenting her. For someone who had been sure that she possessed zilch in the way of theatrical skills, her performance earlier had been remarkable—though she was not proud of the deliberate and determined way in which she had rejected him. She pressed her forehead against the cool glass, seeking solace. She had not wanted to hurt him—nor to reject him. Guy was an appealing and attractive man with many admirable qualities, yet he had a fault, one that she dared not overlook—he was an actor, and, regardless of prophecies of success, acting was a risky affair. But, after three, four, five fraught years she had had more than her fill of risks, and the men who took them!

CHAPTER SIX

ON ARRIVING at Guy's house later in the day, Roxanne had been uneasy. She had dismissed him; did he now intend to reciprocate? If he said to forget about the interior decorating, because he intended to forget her, he could not be blamed. The accusation of her using him possessed a regrettable validity. She did not *want* to use him, but the establishment of some kind of career was crucial to her and Barnaby's future, and having identified such an apt opportunity she was reluctant to let it go.

'Good afternoon,' she smiled when he opened the door.

With grave intent Guy studied her, as though seeking confirmation that her face was as wan as his and that she, too, had dark patches beneath her eyes.

'Grabbed a bit of rest?' he enquired sardonically.

Her smile remained in place. 'Enough,' she replied, then hesitated.

Although the real reason for her rejection was something she preferred not to discuss—start on that theme and she would be forced into a variety of exposures—Roxanne had prepared an explanation for her behaviour last night, and an apology of sorts. Something along the lines of tiredness making her lightheaded and how there had been an air of unreality. No doubt it had affected him, too? Which explained why the goodbye had run amok. Two healthy young people. Alone in the dark. The sex drive. Et cetera. Sorry she had taken so long to come to her senses, but he must be grateful now, if not downright relieved. Impromptu lovemaking might have some fascination in the early hours, but in the glare of day it lay revealed as irresponsible tomfoolery. However, they were adults who knew that these things happened, so they wouldn't make an issue of it, would they? Ha ha.

'Um, about last night. . .' Roxanne began.

'What about it?'

Her heart sank. The words had been terse, unrelenting, bitten out. Whatever she said, it was clear that Guy would not be joining her in hoots of understanding laughter.

'I've been wondering about the left-overs,' she went on quickly. OK, she had lost her nerve, but, after minimal sleep, she was in no fit state to defend herself, especially when for the most part that defence would be a charade. 'If you think you can eat them, please do. However, if not——'

'I can eat *everything*,' he proclaimed.

Roxanne visualised the fridge with its shelves

of food. Gourmet or gourmand, no one could wade their way through that amount, which meant most was destined to be thrown away and wasted. But she and Barnaby could have lived on the left-overs for near enough a week!

'You're sure?' she said dubiously.

His jaw resembled a road-block. 'I'm positive.'

'Brrrrhhh.' Her son's blurt of derision ripped through the air.

Guy frowned at the child, who grinned blithely back, then gradually his mouth spread into a grin, too.

'You're right, buddy boy. Eat that lot and I'll end up the size of a Sumo wrestler,' he said, and the temperature increased by ten degrees. Not to anywhere near tropical, but above the previous arctic. 'Take the left-overs home with you,' he told Roxanne. 'Please.'

She suggested a division of the food and, from then on, everything became easier. As she went around tidying and straightening, Guy lapsed into his normal manner—almost. He talked and joked, and she responded, yet woven into his attitude were doughty threads of caution and detachment. Roxanne suspected that, in addition to all the other minus points he had marked against her, he could now consider her a tease, and he had no time for such women. So why hadn't he declared her *persona non grata*? she wondered. Had the desire to have his house turned into a home been the deciding factor, or his obvious affection for Barnaby? Probably a combination of both.

'Are you planning to be here tomorrow?' he enquired as she prepared to leave.

Roxanne nodded. 'If it's convenient I'd like to make a start undercoating——'

'Go ahead, but don't expect to see me,' Guy intervened. 'And as rehearsals can overrun or be rescheduled without notice, my movements will be erratic for a while.' He took a door-key from the back pocket of his jeans. 'You'd better have that, then you can come and go as you please.'

For the next week, Roxanne did—and for the next week she never saw him. He had left by the time she and Barnaby arrived in the mornings, and although she worked late in the light evenings, occasionally until eight o'clock, he did not once return. Certain his rehearsals could not have started by overrunning to the length of twelve hours a day, *every* day, she decided that he must be avoiding her. Did Guy arrive back, listen for sounds of occupation, and, on hearing them, hightail it to the nearest bar? Maybe he hid behind corners and only emerged when he saw her leave? How juvenile!

Keen for his verdict on the two bedrooms she had painted, Roxanne grudgingly resorted to leaving notes. Did the colours *in situ* meet with his approval? Was he happy with what she had done? The scribbled affirmatives she read the

following day were satisfactory, but not to meet
him face-to-face increasingly annoyed her.

Bedroom curtains were next on the agenda.
Having cut and pinned them over the weekend,
Roxanne spent Monday morning hunched over
her sewing-machine and, after lunch, parcelled
up the finished lengths of sky-blue, grey and
white striped cotton and toted them over.

'The start to yet another week destined to be
spent in splendid isolation,' she muttered as she
wheeled Barnaby into the silent house. Dump-
ing her package, she took hold of his hand. Her
objective today was to hang the curtains and
tackle more glosswork, but first she wanted to
take another look at the first-floor bathroom.
The plaster above the washbasin was pitted and
bumpy, and, on reflection, it seemed doubtful
that painting would be enough of an improvement. 'Come along, Barney,' she said. 'Let's you
and me make a quick inspection, then you can
go out into the garden and play.'

'Me play,' he agreed happily.

Roxanne helped him up the stairs, but as they
reached the landing the little boy broke free.
Running at full tilt, he pushed at the bathroom
door with two hands and jumped inside. She
followed, and was on the threshold when she
came to a startled and abrupt halt.

'Yikes!' she exclaimed.

Naked and dripping and fresh from the
shower, Guy was standing with one foot up on

the wicker laundry-basket, towelling a hairy leg.
So much for splendid isolation! Roxanne
thought, yet could not help thinking that he
looked rather splendid. Water ran in glistening
rivulets over his golden skin, and most of his
skin *was* golden, for now she could see that the
previously admired tan covered all of him—
apart from a narrow strip of white around his
hips. He must have worn ultra-brief swimming
trunks when he had sunbathed, though doubt-
less he had been as at ease in them as he was
now with his nudity. For, where others would
have dashed for the shower cubicle or hastily
draped a towel around themselves, Guy unself-
consciously continued to dry his legs.

'What d'you mean, yikes?' he enquired.

'Er. . .' Hot colour flooded her face. Should
she shield her eyes, or turn her back, or did she
aim to be as nonchalant as he? 'I hadn't
realised. . .I didn't hear. . .you're never usually
around,' Roxanne blustered.

'Don't you recognise a prize backside when
you see one?' Guy asked, with a wink at
Barnaby who was jigging up and down. His
mother might be crippled with embarrassment,
but the toddler was full of glee. His idol had
arrived, at last.

'I beg your pardon?'

'You happen to be ogling the best butt to ever
grace the screen.' He straightened and knotted
the towel around his waist. 'According to the

readers of *Movie Chat* magazine,' he added laconically.

'I'm not ogling. I wasn't,' Roxanne protested, rather too late. Raising her eyes to the wall, she stapled them there. 'I came to take another look at that. It isn't going to be anything special even when it's painted, so I wondered about a false wall. Half a wall. If the mirrors are extended to the full width it could come down to the top of them, then downlighters could be fitted into the jutting out bit, which would provide extra light for shaving. It'd be similar to what was done in the bathroom at my flat,' she gabbled.

'I don't remember your bathroom.'

'Then come and see. We could go over now,' she said, eager to take advantage of his presence.

'Sorry, I can't.'

Roxanne compressed her lips. He was avoiding her again. Damn the man. But she was decorating *his* house for *him* and *he* should take an interest.

'You have a rehearsal?' she queried.

Guy lifted a second towel and began drying his hair. 'No, I've finished for today.'

'You've finished early.'

'I'd had enough,' he said curtly.

'I can't say I'm surprised. A week of rehearsing from morning to late evening would sicken anybody.' Roxanne flicked a curl from her shoulder. 'I assume you were rehearsing until late evening, each evening?'

'No.'

'Ha!' The exclamation burst out.

'We've been stopping around five, but then I've gone straight to the hospital.'

She stared. 'Hospital?' she echoed.

'Emma suffered a stroke last Monday, though fortunately it was slight. She's due back at the home this afternoon. That's where I'm off to now.'

'Is she—has she recovered?' Roxanne faltered.

'She's fine, apart from a slight twisting of her mouth which the doctors say will soon go. However, it doesn't stop her complaining— about the nurses, the food, and about me,' Guy added drily.

'You're still getting it in the neck?'

'I am. Even though she appears to derive little pleasure from our meetings, she reckons I should have spent longer at her bedside, that the evenings weren't enough. I explained that I have other commitments, but——' He gave a wry smile. 'I'm sorry our contact's been second-hand of late,' he continued, 'but I'd like to take this opportunity to say I think what you're doing is great.'

For days Roxanne had been desperate to hear his praise, yet now it passed her by. She felt ashamed, and disgusted with herself. Like the old lady, she had been full of grumbles, and, like the old lady's, her grumbles had been selfish and unfair.

'Thanks,' she muttered distractedly.

His hair dried and combed, Guy walked past her and through to his bedroom with Barnaby in tow.

'About cash,' he called. 'You must have already paid out a fair sum for various items and I'd like to settle my account as we go.'

Distraction fled. Snap!—her mind was concentrated beautifully. Roxanne had financed the initial costs of the refurbishment in the same way she financed all her expenses, but much torturous economical fine tuning would be avoided if he made a speedy reimbursement.

'Thanks,' she said, trying to sound casual, but could not resist adding, 'If you want to clear the outstanding amount now, I have the receipts in my bag.'

'I'll take a look at them in a minute,' he promised.

Beyond the bedroom door she caught sight of Barnaby being tickled, giggling, running around, and of Guy coming and going as he assembled underwear, a shirt, dark trousers, a tie. For a moment Roxanne stood there, then, wary of being accused of ogling again, she went downstairs. When he joined her in the study, the accounts were neatly laid out on his desk.

'There are discounts of fifteen or twenty per cent on most of these,' Guy remarked, riffling through them. He leant back in his chair. 'How did you manage that?'

'I didn't manage anything,' Roxanne said, in indignant defence against what had sounded like a charge of malpractice. 'At the moment, it's the summer sales, and if you shop around it's possible to pick up some fantastic bargains. That's one of the reasons why I was so keen to get started. For example, the coconut fibre twist we decided to use in your kitchen is on offer at half the normal price. All the fabrics and carpets at the flat were bought in the sales, and most of the paint,' she carried on, determined to illustrate that her common-sense tactics were tried and tested. 'There's a DIY store in Hammersmith which sells end-of-range colours at give-away prices, and I used them in the bathroom, the hall, and all three bedrooms.'

He took a calculator from the desk-drawer and began adding up totals. 'Then your place really was decorated on a shoestring,' he muttered, jabbing away.

Roxanne glared at his bent head. 'You thought I'd lied?'

'No, but——' Guy looked up. 'What did your husband think about it?' he enquired.

'To be frank, my style wasn't his style. Oh, he assured me I'd done a magificent job, and when other people enthused he was always the first to agree that it was wonderful, but I knew he found the flat much too. . .plain. Hamish preferred his home to be furnished in the Versailles mode,' she said, when he looked surprised. 'The Belgravia house was thick with brocade curtains, oil-paintings, crystal chandeliers. Watered silk covered the walls, everything that could be gilded was gilded, and if you took two steps you found your path obstructed by an ornate lamp or an occasional table crowded with silverware and porcelain.' She shuddered. 'Yuck!'

Guy hooked an arm around the clamouring Barnaby and sat him on his knee. 'Do I hear the generation gap talking?'

'No, you don't!' she replied quickly. Too quickly. 'People have different tastes, that's all.'

'Why did you marry Hamish?'

Roxanne collected the accounts into a neat bundle. 'Because I loved him.'

'How did you come to fall in love with a man who was so much older?' he asked, sharpshooter style.

Her insides clenched. All of a sudden she felt heavy, as though her veins were clogged with lead.

'You make him sound ancient,' she prevaricated.

'If Hamish were alive, he'd be in his fifties.'

'Just,' Roxanne agreed unwillingly.

'Maybe that isn't ancient, but the age difference is still too great.'

'In *your* opinion!'

'In most people's.'

'Hamish may have been older, but he was tremendously fit,' Roxanne declared. 'He exercised daily, he jogged, he paid attention to his diet. He was trimmer than most younger men. If you've seen him you must have noticed his vitality, but he also had bags of personality, and charm, and——'

'He was a handsome devil,' Guy said as she rummaged around for another recommendation. He produced a cheque book from the desk and, after cautioning Barnaby to keep still, wrote out a cheque which he handed to her. 'How did you meet Hamish?' he enquired.

'Through my father. They—they knew each other.'

'Your father was a lame duck?'

The cheque fluttered from her hand. Why should Guy suggest that? she wondered, bending to retrieve it. How did he know? He couldn't. She had only mentioned her father once, or was it twice? Whichever, she had given no hint of his. . .weakness.

Face flushed, Roxanne stood upright. 'A lame duck?' she repeated stiltedly.

'You told me he'd been ill, plus you stressed Hamish's kindness—but perhaps I've put two and two together and come up with five?'

Guy's addition was as accurate as if he had used his calculator, but should she tell him? The idea was tempting. For so long she had kept silent, but maybe those exposures—some of them, at least—*needed* to be exposed? Maybe it would be healthier? Maybe talking about her father would be therapeutic? Yet as she tucked the cheque away in her bag, Roxanne frowned. If she unburdened herself the dam of secrecy would be breached, and wouldn't there then be a danger of her blabbing again? She trusted Guy not to repeat anything, but on the next occasion her confidant might not be so reliable.

'You have. Ready for the garden?' she asked Barnaby. 'He plays out there most of the time,' she explained as the little boy scrambled from Guy's knee.

'So you spend your day running up and down the stairs making sure he's OK?'

'And admiring the latest pile of earth or vast hole,' Roxanne said wryly. 'He goes home caked in dirt, but wreathed in smiles. Keep your fingers crossed that the sun continues to shine.'

The sun shone. Another day passed. More woodwork was painted, further soil mountains constructed and craters dug. Happier now that she knew Guy was not avoiding her, Roxanne settled into a routine, and was surprised when, on letting herself into the house the following morning, he called a hello. As her son rushed off in the direction of his voice, she walked behind and found him finishing breakfast in the kitchen.

'Is anything the matter?' Roxanne enquired, after the initial exchange of greetings. Two days ago, she had noticed a tension in the set of Guy's jaw, a tightness around his mouth, and had attributed them to the pressures of Emma's illness. The old lady might be a cussed character, yet he took his responsibilities seriously and had, she knew, been in constant touch with her son—who, it had to be said, did not appear overly distressed. Now, with his charge out of hospital and out of danger, those pressures should have slackened, but a grimness lurked beneath his smile. 'Is it Emma? Has she——'

'Emma's fine.'

Roxanne looked at the clock; it was gone ten. 'Don't you have a rehearsal?'

'Not today.'

'Why not?'

Guy expelled a heavy sigh. 'Because everything's become so high-powered and fraught that if we didn't have a break someone would snap. Probably me.'

'Isn't the play going well?' she asked in surprise.

After listening to Prue praise his talent, it had never occurred to her that he could hit problems, not serious ones. She had—naïvely, she now realised—regarded his acting ability as all-powerful and easily won.

'Part is. Part isn't,' he said briefly, and reached down to hoist Barnaby into his arms. 'However, even though I'm taking time off I've still been active. Come along. I've something to show the pair of you.'

Down the hall, across the living-room, and out through the french windows, he went to where a sandpit had been built in one corner of the garden, adjacent to the house. Enclosed by a low wall of bricks, it was equipped with a generous supply of buckets and spades.

He stood the little boy down. 'Get to it, Barney,' he grinned.

With a hoot of delight, the toddler ran and dumped himself on top of the pile of yellow sand and began excitedly collecting the toys around him. Which should he play with first? The scarlet bucket? The green spade? Did he excavate, or make a sand pie?

As Roxanne watched, a rush of sentiment brought unexpected tears to her eyes. 'Thank you,' she said, and, reaching up, she pressed her lips to Guy's cheek.

'More,' he said.

'More?' she echoed, abruptly uncertain beneath his brown-eyed gaze.

When he had spoken of an attraction between them, he had been right. Whatever his doubts about her, however much she might ignore it, whenever they were together there *was* a throb in the air. A sensual throb.

He raised his brows. 'More,' he murmured.

Roxanne kissed him on the mouth—what else

could she do? It was a friendly kiss, uncompromisingly bland, yet when she drew back the touch of his lips against hers lingered like a poignant memory—tender, zinging, warm.

'The sand wasn't here yesterday, so when. . .?' she asked, her heart thudding wildly.

'I arranged for it to be delivered at the crack of dawn, then got busy building the wall.'

She grinned. 'Sounds as if you've done a day's work already.'

Guy wiped imaginary sweat from his brow. 'Feels like it. I was recovering with a cup of coffee, but I could do with another one. How about you?'

'I ought to make a start on my painting, but ——' Roxanne smiled. 'Yes, please.'

'Remember how we were talking about your husband the other day,' he enquired, when they were sitting on the sofa nursing steaming mugs, 'and I asked what he felt about you doing up the flat? You gave me his reaction to the interior decorating, but what I actually meant was, what did he think about you doing it on a shoestring?'

Roxanne picked at a blob of dried paint on the knee of her jeans. 'He was pleased. Just because he had money in the bank, it didn't mean——'

'But was there anything in the bank?' Guy cut in. 'You've said very little about Hamish,' he went on, when her head swung round and she stared at him, 'but in addition to picking up mixed signals about your relationship——'

'What mixed signals?' she demanded.

'You reckon he was kind, generous, full of charm, yet when I suggested you marrying again I got a very dusty answer. Why? If you had such a good experience the first time around, surely you'd be willing to repeat it?'

'Perhaps it's because I don't consider any other man could take his place,' Roxanne said swiftly.

'Perhaps.' Her remark was left to ride. 'There are various things on the financial side which don't fit. For instance, one minute the two of you are languishing in the rarefied reaches of Belgravia, and the next you go down-market to——'

'The flat isn't down-market!'

'By comparison it is. I agree it's a valuable property in anyone's terms, but it can only be worth a third of the house. You also mentioned porcelain, silverware and oil-paintings, but those seem to have disappeared, too. Hamish enjoyed living in style—you said so—and he flaunted it; I remember seeing the Belgravia pad in a Sunday colour supplement. Suddenly he quits, and in stealth, because as far as I'm aware his selling up was never mentioned in the Press. So, when everything's considered——' Guy took a mouthful of coffee '—it's not difficult to work out that the move took place in order to acquire ready cash.'

Roxanne sighed. As he had been right about her father, so he was right now—and again she was tempted to tell him the truth. Yet as she had hesitated before, so she hung back now. The truth showed Hamish up in a bad light, and, if only for Barnaby's sake, wasn't it her duty to keep quiet?

'I overheard Athol,' Guy said when she frowned and scratched at the paint blob again.

She cast him a wary look. 'What did you hear?'

'Just a few words like skint and busted. At the time I assumed he was referring to himself, but now I believe he meant you—or your husband. Same thing. If, when he died, all Hamish left you was the flat, then that would explain why you were so keen to have the *Assignment Paris* fees, and why earning your own money is of such importance now.'

Roxanne gazed out into the garden where her son contentedly played. 'Athol *was* talking about me—and Hamish,' she admitted. 'You see, almost every show he'd backed over the eight or nine years before he died had bombed.'

Guy frowned at her. 'Are you sure?' he demanded. 'OK, only one production in five is reckoned to make a profit, but——'

'I'm sure. Oh, I know he was supposed to have the golden touch, and when he first invested in the threatre he did have a spectacular run. But one of the conditions Hamish insisted upon before backing a show was that his involvement must not be publicised without his permission, and he only gave that if the venture proved to be a money-spinner—then he had his name shouted from the rooftops. He claimed that, by maintaining the aura of success, he was making certain all the best opportunities would be brought to his door.' Roxanne sipped from her mug. 'Also, thanks to his reputation, it was always assumed that whenever anything *was* a hit Hamish Dunn had invested. Sometimes he hadn't, but he didn't put the record straight, and when reporters asked about failures he'd only own up to one or two minor ones.'

Guy considered what she had said. 'Surely he must have saved money in the good years?' he enquired.

'He did, but though backing shows gave him an instant high it didn't last long, so as soon as he'd put cash into one he began searching around for the next. And the more failures he had, the more impulsive he became. He forgot about weighing up the pros and cons, and blindly sponsored all kinds of events which no one ever got to hear about—here, in America, Australia, on the continent.'

'He stopped playing safe?'

'I don't believe he ever had; it wasn't in his

nature. So, as rapidly as the millions had accumulated, they diminished.' A shadow crossed her face. 'And, as I've said, Hamish was generous. He'd lend money, big chunks of money, and never ask for it back. I told him he should, but——' She gave a bleak shrug.

'Then how have you and Barney been surviving?' Guy demanded.

'Through the sale of jewellery and some clothes. I never wanted expensive fashions, nor asked to be showered with gems, but he insisted,' Roxanne said wistfully.

'And when did he tell you he was broke?'

'He didn't.'

'Never?' Guy protested.

'Never ever. When he raised the move from Belgravia, I realised something was wrong and I tackled him, but although he admitted to losing some money he dismissed it as insignificant.'

'And you believed him?'

Roxanne wrapped a strand of dark hair around and around her finger. 'No, but he insisted on managing our finances alone, and he was so much older than me and had years of business experience, so I didn't feel I was in any position to call him a liar. I suggested I returned to modelling—as well as the extra income helping, I was also bored with staying at home—but Hamish had set ideas on what was "done" or "not done", with no space for manoeuvre in between, and a working wife was unacceptable.

I tried to persuade him, but the concept of discussing things with a woman and reaching a mutual decision was alien to him,' she said, and stopped. She had been aware of these traits before her marriage, so what was the point in bleating about them now? If Hamish had not been the ideal partner, she only had herself to blame. 'You're free today, so suppose we go over and look at my bathroom?' Roxanne suggested, with a hasty grind of conversational gears.

For a moment Guy hesitated, then he smiled. 'If you wish,' he replied.

Prising Barnaby from the sandpit was not easy. No matter how much his hero coaxed and swung the little boy high in the air, for once he went unheeded, and it was only Roxanne's bribe of a toffee lollipop which finally enticed him away.

'Just as well our destination is the bathroom,' she remarked as she unlocked the door to the flat. She grimaced at her son's brown-rimmed mouth and stickily waving fingers. 'First stop, soap and water.'

She was in the middle of extracting Barnaby, at arm's length, from his pushchair when the telephone rang.

'Answer it,' Guy said as she dithered. 'I can deal with buddy boy.'

Her caller was Mohammed Hussein, calling to tell her that Fatima was on the brink of marriage.

After months of negotiations, arrangements between the two families had been finalised, and now the ceremony was only days away.

'Salim hinted a wedding could be in the air, but that's wonderful.' Roxanne smiled, watching Guy steer his ward down the hall. 'I hope she'll be very happy.'

'To a certain extent that depends on you,' Mr Hussein replied.

'Me?'

'Her husband-to-be works for a shipping line and, out of the blue, his company has decided to post him to their London branch. Regardless of the myth about people from my country, he is not wealthy, and, this being the case, I felt duty-bound to tell the young couple that I might be able to offer them accommodation.'

'Here,' she said, before he could get any further.

'That is correct.' There was a taut pause. 'I have no wish to inconvenience you, but you did say you could leave whenever I asked, and——'

'I can. It's no problem,' Roxanne proclaimed, though her legs had turned to jelly and she needed to sit down. 'I'll tell my brother to expect me at the end of the week.'

'There's no rush,' Mr Hussein hastened to assure her.

She frowned. In her opinion, after occupying his property free of charge for more than two years, speed was essential. Her landlord had been so cordial and undemanding, it would be wrong to take liberties by clinging on now. She must go, and quickly. Her sense of fair play insisted on it.

'The flat'll be available by Sunday,' Roxanne told him. 'I'll leave the keys with the porter and arrange for the various meters to be read. I'll write down the days for putting out the rubbish, and——' the full force of what was happening hit, and her mind went blank '—and everything,' she finished lamely.

Mr Hussein chatted on for a few minutes, then, promising to be in touch again before she left, he said goodbye.

Roxanne replaced the receiver and sat with her head in her hands. In the background there were sounds of Barnaby, now washed and in his bedroom, rummaging through his toy-box in search of some special toy. She trembled. In four days' time that bedroom would no longer be his. In four days' time the pair of them would be homeless. Of no fixed abode. Vagabonds.

'I thought your brother lived abroad,' Guy said, coming back down the hall.

'He does. Paul lives in Sydney, Australia,' she added dully.

'And you're intending to go there?'

'No. No.' Roxanne looked up. 'You overheard?'

'I couldn't help it.' He gazed angrily around.

'So—damned Hamish didn't even leave you this place?'

'Yes, damned Hamish did!' she flared, but her rebellion was short-lived. 'However, he also left debts which needed to be paid.'

'What sort of debts?' Guy demanded.

'There were several big loans which had to be settled, bills for his new car, half a dozen expensive suits, my clothes, my jewellery.'

He swore. 'So the things he'd bought for you, he'd bought on credit?'

Roxanne nodded. 'At the time I assumed he could afford it, but. . .' Briefly, she described the situation after her husband's death and how his friend had come to the rescue, then detailed the telephone call. 'I've always known my residence must end some time,' she completed, 'but Mr Hussein never once mentioned selling the flat, and so I'd hoped to hang on until I'd managed to earn enough to be able to set myself up somewhere else.'

Frowning, Guy hooked his thumbs into his belt. 'If you had the fees from *Assignment Paris* you'd be able to set yourself up somewhere else,' he muttered. A nerve pulsed in his temple. 'I'll get in touch with the television people and tell them——'

'Don't you dare!' she said fiercely.

'Rox——'

'If you tell them to go ahead with that asinine series, *I* shall veto it.'

'But——'

'No!'

He cast her a speculative glance. 'You've had a change of heart?'

'I've looked at the situation sensibly and from every angle,' she rejoined, 'and I agree that *Assignment Paris* is better left to moulder. Did you ever contact the supporting actors about bona fide payments?' Roxanne enquired, suddenly curious.

'Yes, though not in person. It promised to be a lengthy job, so my agent insisted his secretary would do it for me. I understand there was some hassle finding names and addresses, but in the end she got in touch with them all.'

'And?' she asked when he hesitated.

'The majority were happy to say "good riddance" and walk away, but three were going through hard times and so I've sent them a cheque each. However,' Guy said slowly, 'that doesn't mean *Assignment Paris* can't be repeated.'

'Over my dead body! Karen'll be happy to take me and Barney—for a month or so until I sort something out, and I will. My gold chains should be worth——'

'This Karen has a house?' he cut in.

'A flat.'

'Size?'

'One bedroom, but there's a folding settee in

the living-room,' Roxanne rushed on, 'so we'll be perfectly comfortable.'

'Now pull the other leg.'

'We *will*.'

'Like hell,' he rejected as Barnaby ran up to thrust a clockwork car into his hands.

'So what do you suggest I do?' she demanded.

'I'm not suggesting, I'm telling.' Briskly Guy turned the key. 'You and Barney are coming to stay with me.'

CHAPTER SEVEN

ALTHOUGH, somewhere at the back of her mind, Roxanne knew that going to live in the house of a young heterosexual actor who made the air *throb* could not be classed as the wisest of manoeuvres, she did not argue. Any uprooting had been firmly placed in the future, and its abrupt reversal to here and now stunned.

How would she manage the transfer? she wondered as Guy sent the toy car speeding down the hall. Mr Hussein had bought the flat furnished, but on the understanding that specified items belonged to her—so what should she do about the Chinese screen, a grandfather clock, the silver cutlery and other such things? A mixture of Ledgard family treasures and wedding gifts, she regarded them as sacrosanct and, thus far, had refused to sell them—but would there be enough room at the Chelsea house? And what about clothes, favourite books, Barnaby's cot, highchair and toys? If she did take everything, how could she ferry the goods over? Roxanne fretted. Could she entice a taxi-driver to act as beast of burden? How many journeys would be involved? How much was the move going to *cost*?

'There's nothing to worry about,' Guy declared when she tentatively voiced her fears. 'Chris is a director of a firm of wholesale stationers which runs a fleet of vans, so I'll tell him he's volunteered to help shift your worldly goods and to report, with transport, on Saturday morning. After bringing that Athol character to the party, he owes us both one. A big one,' he said cryptically. 'As for space, I'll get the council to remove those pieces of junk which we decided weren't worth saving. They need to be dumped anyway.' He spread his hands and smiled. 'It'll be easy.'

Saturday dawned bright and sunny. Through the busy streets, the van travelled being loaded and emptied, loaded and emptied, until, eventually, the flat was clear of Roxanne's possessions. A break was taken for sandwiches and beer, then the two men began heaving everything up to the allocated bedrooms. As Roxanne got busy with her unpacking, Chris departed in the van and, in due course, Guy departed to the Chinese take-away. Dinner was eaten and, while her host cleared the dishes, Roxanne bathed her son and settled him in his cot. A victim of the day's excitement, Barnaby was asleep in two minutes flat.

'Thank you for everything,' Roxanne smiled as she joined Guy in the garden. The evening was balmy, the air heavy with the fragrance of blossoms, and he was relaxing on the pew—

which now did duty as a garden bench. 'You were right, moving was easy—well, relatively painless.'

'Told you,' he grinned, 'and, yes, I *do* realise it'll all need to be gone through again when you leave in a month or so. As you informed Chris, *ad nauseum*! Likewise that you'd be paving your own way.'

She sat down beside him. 'I didn't want him to get the wrong idea.'

'You don't want Chris to think we're lovers?' Brown eyes met hers in a level look. 'Hard luck, Rox, he does. Ditto the porter, and Suzi and Kim, and all your neighbours who waved you off.'

Lovers? The word was emotive. It brought all kinds of disturbing images to mind.

'No, no, it's not that,' she said, frowning.

'You don't mind if we're generally rumoured to be living in sin—at least, for the next four weeks?'

'Not if you don't.'

'I don't.' Guy regarded her curiously. 'So what do you mind?'

'I—I wouldn't like Chris, or anyone, to think I can't afford to move on. I can, it's simply a matter of having the time to consolidate my resources and decide——'

'Let me get this straight,' he cut in. 'What you're hung up on is people realising you're strapped for cash? You don't want it to leak out that your husband left you damn-all?'

Roxanne lowered her head. 'No.'

'But it's nothing to be ashamed of,' Guy protested. 'Being a theatrical angel or, in Hamish's case, an archangel, is a high-risk venture. Everyone's aware of that. Granted, he wasn't as sensible as he should have been and so he lost out, but it's hardly a disgrace of cosmic proportions.'

Her head came up. 'No one must know,' she said, her tone suddenly fevered. 'It must never become public knowledge.'

For a long moment his eyes held hers, their expression dark and intense, then he tilted his head and gazed up into the sky. A colourful sunset was bringing the summer's day to a close, and the heavens were painted with soft pinks, greys and golds.

'Now *I* have a back-up idea for if my career should hit the skids,' Guy said with a grin. 'I shall go into the house removal business.'

Entrapped in her thoughts, Roxanne had assumed his to be on the same track and was unprepared for this change of direction.

'Sorry?'

'Sometimes you get lucky and sometimes you don't.'

She shot him a look. No further mention had been made of his rehearsals—and in the upheaval of moving there had been no time to ask—but now both his voice and his grin were strained.

'Is the play still causing problems?' she enquired.

'It's not the play which is the problem, it's me.' Guy jabbed an angry thumb into his chest. '*Me!*'

'Why? How?'

He shook a dismissive head. 'It's something I have to work out for myself.'

'Tell me,' Roxanne appealed. 'I'm interested.'

'No, you're not. You're not interested in acting. You think it's a bloody ridiculous way to earn a living, and you want to know something—so do I!' He frowned, realising he was being overly aggressive. 'I'm finding it difficult to get into the character I'm playing, that's all.'

'Explain.'

'Why?' he said rebelliously.

'Because I'm asking you to. Please.'

Again Guy studied the sunset. 'When I took the role,' he began reluctantly, 'I came out with bravura statements like "needing to stretch myself" and how acting is all about taking chances. At the time I thought I believed them, though I suspect from the start I had my doubts, but now——' he closed his eyes and opened them again '—now, to be honest, Rox, I'm scared. Thirty-three years old and scared to death, scared of pretending to be someone who never existed, ain't that something to headbang about?' he said, in fierce self-contempt. 'It's not as though governments are going to fall if I mess up. There won't be a total eclipse of the sun, nor will the fountains run with blood!'

He was sitting with one hand clenched around his knee, the knuckles white, and Roxanne covered it with her own.

'But great things are expected of you, and you are putting your career on the line,' she said gently.

He looked down at their fingers, hers tapered and fair-skinned lying atop his, square and brown. 'I guess,' he sighed. 'The films I've done this year are good, but if the play's a disaster I don't suppose anyone'll give a damn about them.' He hooked his little finger around hers. 'Fear's reckoned to motivate, but on this occasion it's brought my creative instincts to a full stop.'

'What's his name?' Roxanne enquired.

'Who?'

'The man who doesn't exist.'

'Oh. Jonas Willoughby.'

'What does he do? What kind of personality does he have? How old is he?' she questioned.

'He's a lawyer. He's smart, sophisticated, full of charisma—and he has a calculating streak a mile wide. In the first half of the play he's a prosecuting counsel, amusing yet merciless, but in the second he's in the dock himself, accused of murder and desperately attempting to extricate himself. In Act One he's thirty-four or -five and I've got that taped, but when the action starts up again he's aged ten years, and——' Guy came to a halt. 'Let me explain how I work. I start off externally by getting images of the physical way I want the character to be, then it seeps into me and I become it. Him.' He frowned. 'I hope that doesn't sound too heavy, but it's the way I do it.'

'You base the outward look on a person you've met?'

'Sometimes it's one person. Sometimes it can be an amalgam.'

'And Jonas being middle-aged is the stumbling block?'

'It's not the age. I've played older men before, successfully. No, the tricky thing is that although, in Act Two, Jonas is forty-five or so, he has a deep aversion to being that old and fights it—subtly, not blatantly—but although I've been playing him as older acting younger, it won't jell. I wind up with him being damn near identical to ten years earlier.' Guy heaved a sigh. 'Somehow I have to make the man's true age *felt*, not seen in the grey at his temples, nor heard in references to the past. And it'll happen—it had better.' He released her hand. 'It's getting dark. Let's go inside.'

'I assume Jonas is vain?' Roxanne said as they went into the living-room.

Guy might be content for the subject to die, but she was determined to keep it alive. He had eased her problems, and now—although it would be painful, if not harrowing—she had recognised an opportunity to ease his.

'Vain, and obsessed with the face he presents to the world.' After switching on a table-lamp, he dropped down in the corner of the sofa opposite her. 'Or, I should say, the façade.'

Roxanne moistened her lips. 'I know who you should base him on.'

'Who?'

'Hamish.'

He shot her a look. 'Hamish was vain?'

'Yes——' she took a breath '—and obsessed with how others saw him, and with his age. Every day he exercised, yet there was no pleasure involved; it was a grim fanatical slog to keep the years at bay. He was also calculating, not only in his dealings with the Press, but——'

'There's no need to tell me this,' Guy said quietly.

'There is. I'd like to help you, if I can.' Roxanne gave a pale smile. 'I'd also like to help myself, by facing up to the truth about Hamish—and about me. I've relived those nine months we were married a hundred times in my head and gone through a thousand emotions, but I've never once spoken about them, not honestly. I've always been so sensitive to everyone's disapproval of our relationship, that whenever Hamish's name is mentioned I automatically leap to his defence.' She caught her lip between her teeth. 'And—and the thought of being disloyal has troubled me. But if I say out loud what I really think, maybe it'll clarify matters, lay a few ghosts, force me to accept the reality. Guy, I want to talk,' she said urgently, then frowned. 'If you don't mind listening?'

A muscle tightened in his jaw. 'I don't mind.'

'It could take a long time,' she warned.

He grinned. 'In that case, I'd better bring us some wine.'

A bottle and glasses were collected from the kitchen, and wine poured.

'Before I can tell you about Hamish, I need to explain about my father,' Roxanne said when she had taken a mouthful. 'I said he was ill at the time of *Assignment Paris*, but——' her sigh was deep-felt '—what I didn't say was that his illness was gambling. Dad had always enjoyed putting a pound or two on the odd horse, but after my mother died he started to bet on a regular basis. For a long time my brother and I had no idea, and when we did discover we regarded it as a hobby, a way of finding some release from his pain.'

'Your father was very broken up about your mother?' Guy asked.

'Devastated. Throughout thirty years of marriage, they'd been very much in love. It can happen,' she said whimsically. 'However, as time went by Dad began taking days off work to go to the races, and became a member of a couple of gaming clubs. Paul and I weren't comfortable with it, but whenever losses were mentioned they were small, and as Dad also spoke of wins from time to time it sounded as though he could be breaking even. So we didn't feel we had any real grounds for complaint.'

'But he wasn't breaking even?'

'No, he was losing week after week, month after month, on and on and on—though it took almost three years for the situation to reach crisis point.' She shuddered. 'Then, in the space of a week, life as Paul and I had known it collapsed. My father was an accountant, and first he was sacked for fiddling the books and filching cash to finance his bets. Two days later, the building society served notice that they intended to repossess our house—because Dad had taken out a second loan and was grossly behind with the repayments. And, finally, he produced a batch of bills from various betting shops and casinos demanding payment, or else. Paul and I believed he'd joined two clubs, but it turned out he had membership of several.' Roxanne ran a slow finger around the rim of her glass. 'In those three years my father had gambled away over a hundred thousand pounds.'

Guy muttered an oath. 'What the hell did you do?'

'Apart from have a nervous breakdown? My

earnings were high and I'd saved, so I was able to pay off the building society. Then we sold the house and moved into rented accommodation, which enabled us to pay back the money Dad had taken from his company and settle the gambling debts. The rented place was small,' she said, recalling the cramped rooms, 'but mainly it was just my father and me living there, so we managed. Paul's a couple of years younger than me, and he was away at university,' she explained. 'When everything had been settled, we insisted that Dad must seek professional help, and he was so full of remorse and desperate to make amends that he couldn't agree quickly enough.'

'But?' Guy asked, when distress tightened her features.

'For a while the counselling did seem to work, and Dad swore he was a reformed character, but all he'd done was become devious. Gambling was a drug and he needed regular fixes. He'd found another job, though it didn't pay much—without a reference he'd had to take whatever he could find—so to support his addiction he ran up more bills, he lied, he stole money from me and Paul, and heaven knows who else. All his life he'd been an upright, law-abiding citizen, but now his character completely changed. Morals didn't count for anything, he *must* place bets.' Roxanne swallowed down the lump which had formed in her throat. 'By the time of *Assignment Paris*, club managers were hounding us, and I was terrified to answer the phone in case it was someone announcing that he'd lifted their wallet and they were taking him to court.'

Guy reached across and squeezed her hand. 'Now I know why your mind was miles away.'

'I seemed to be enveloped in a fog of fear about what Dad would do next and I couldn't focus on anything else.' She scraped together a smile. 'Not even *zee sexy gendarme*. My father was taken to court,' Roxanne carried on, 'though not until several months later. That's how I met Hamish. Dad had somehow wangled membership of a classy Mayfair casino, run up a bill, and failed to pay it. By then my savings were long gone and we were living off my income, so I made an appointment and begged for time, but they refused. When the case came up, Dad and I went along and——'

'Your brother didn't go?' Guy interrupted.

'No.' Tears stung, blurring her vision. 'Shortly after graduating Paul was offered a job in Australia and—and he took it.' She blinked. 'However, when we arrived at the court precinct it was to find Hamish settling the debt.'

'So the case was dropped?'

'Yes.'

'Nice to have friends,' he remarked.

'But Dad and Hamish weren't friends. They hardly knew each other, though I didn't realise it at the time. I dumbly assumed the debt had been paid out of straightforward kindness, but I discovered later, much later, that Hamish had seen me when I'd called at the casino and—and decided he wanted to get to know me.'

'Which he did,' Guy said drily.

'But I made it so easy. You've heard of women patients falling in love with their doctors out of gratitude? I fell for him in much the same way. True, he was personable and easy to get on with, and all that stuff, but I allowed myself to be ruled by emotion——' Roxanne raised despairing eyes to his '—only it was the *wrong* emotion!'

He squeezed her hand again. 'You were going through some pretty emotional times,' he murmured.

She nodded. 'For what seemed like forever I'd lived in fear and with an awful sense of isolation because, although Paul had initially been supportive, after Dad broke his promises and started gambling again he didn't want to know. Try to talk and he walked away.' Her grey eyes misted over. 'Then Hamish breezed in, decisive, positive and ready to dictate the score—and suddenly Dad *was* a reformed character. After paying his debt, Hamish gave him a good talking-to,' she explained, 'and he never gambled again.'

Guy's brows rose. 'Your father kicked the habit overnight?'

'He did. At the time it seemed as if Hamish was responsible, though now I think it was the shock of attending court which showed him the error of his ways. However, I was overwhelmed with thanks and, in consequence, so *suggestible*,' she said, in weary self-reproach, 'that when Hamish proposed, I agreed.'

'The age difference wasn't a factor?'

'Surprising though it may seem, no. OK, I thought about it, but in a very superficial way. You see, everything happened so quickly, and Hamish was this white knight, my saviour, and—and he did give the impression of being young. It was only when I knew him better that I realised it was——' Roxanne searched for an apt description '—a bogus youth characterised by activity. You remember how he entered a room, all smiles and with arms swinging? He used to brace himself on the threshold like a sprinter on a block, then march in with long strides as if he'd been summoned by royalty to collect his knighthood. And he was perpetually raking back his hair. He had thick, wavy hair, but in addition to drawing attention to it I'm sure he raked it back because he believed the gesture was youthful. Certainly it wasn't spontaneous. Not much was with Hamish. He needed glasses for reading,' she went on, 'but he never simply wore them. They were either perched on the end of his nose or he was waving them around, as if to prove he didn't really need them. It was quite endearing in a way.' Roxanne gave a rueful smile. 'I tried to tease him about it, but he wasn't receptive. Hamish hated being teased or shown up in any way. Normally he had a good sense of humour, but put him in a situation where he felt his dignity was threatened and he became very prissy.' She expelled a breath. 'He was full of contradictions.'

'Most of us are,' Guy observed.

'Although Hamish had this youth fetish, he never dressed young—as in casual,' Roxanne continued, then suddenly she chuckled. 'He'd never have worn Mickey Mouse shorts!'

'You should see my Superman ones.'

'Spare me!'

'You reckon I ought to buy a pair of Y-fronts for on stage?' Guy grinned.

'Plain white ones, and a pair of spectacles.'

'I might.' He slung a long leg over the low arm of the sofa. 'Was the age gap much of a problem to you after your marriage?'

'Yes, though not at first. Initially it was enough to wallow in the security Hamish had provided.' Roxanne looked at him. 'And I do mean security, not money. It was wonderful to be free of Dad's gambling, his pilfering, the nasty phone calls. It was wonderful to be able to relax. The stupid thing is, I was so busy giving thanks for the demise of gambling-inspired catastrophes that the significance of Hamish's knowing my father via the casino passed me by.'

'He liked to throw the dice, too?'

'On occasion, though when that particular Lady Luck ran out he could meet his losses. But I knew he put money, big money, into shows, and if I'd had any sense I would've realised that all I'd done was exchange one kind of speculator for another.' Roxanne swirled the wine in her glass. 'I can't decide whether, in dismissing the fact, I was being an optimist or an ostrich. And when I think of how Hamish warned my father against the dangers of gambling——' Her eyes went skywards.

Guy frowned. 'I take it that if you'd been in a steadier frame of mind his being an impresario would have stopped you from marrying him?'

'Definitely. After riding the roller-coaster of uncertainty once, the last thing I'd planned was to climb aboard a second time. Guaranteed reliability of life-style was what I wanted then——' she straightened her shoulders '—and it's what I intend to have now. So there I was, wallowing in security—fake——' she said pithily '—and being grateful. When Hamish suggested I give up modelling, and when he started to buy me fancy clothes and jewellery, I didn't resist too much because my whole aim was to please him. And I did.' A tinge of acidity entered her voice. 'As a young wife who devoted herself to his needs and who looked like a fashion plate, I was the perfect accessory.'

'Part of the image?'

'Definitely,' Roxanne said again. 'But it wasn't long before I started to resent being paraded and, more particularly, when people remarked on how similar I was to Hamish's first wife. He'd never shown me her photograph—deliberately, I imagine—but I insisted and immediately I realised what everyone meant, because I was her double. I also realised that Hamish's paying Dad's bill and *then* meeting me—Janet reincarnated—had to be too much of a coincidence, and when I asked he confessed he'd been at the casino the day I'd visited.'

Guy poured second glasses of wine. 'He'd zeroed in because you resembled her?'

'Yes, and that's why he married me. Oh, Hamish was fond of me,' she consented when he made a protest, 'but I'm sure our marriage was an attempt to recapture the times he'd enjoyed with her.'

'When he was young?'

'Young *and* successful. You see, just as my mother's death triggered off my father's troubles, so, after Janet died, Hamish's flair for picking winning shows began to go haywire too. He must have been in the thick of financial problems when we met, and I figure he planned on my restoring his luck.' She sighed. 'But our marriage was ill-omened from the start.'

'Had to be,' Guy said grimly, 'when he'd gone into it for cock-eyed reasons.'

'But I'd done the same!' Roxanne protested. 'Very soon I was forced to admit that—that even if I liked him, I didn't love him, and that I'd mishandled the major relationship that anyone has in their life.' She rubbed agitated fingers across her brow. 'I felt so guilty, so angry with myself, so deeply ashamed—and I still do.'

'Sweetheart, you were young, influenced and confused by your feelings, and—everyone makes mistakes.'

'Such a *big* one?' she wailed.

'Until that point you'd lead a relatively sheltered life?' Guy demanded.

'Yes.'

'Then Hamish sweeps in—a mature, forceful, jet-setting character—and you're flattered when he takes an interest?'

Roxanne nibbled at a lip. 'I suppose so.'

'And he sweeps you off your feet?'

'I suppose,' she said again.

'Then don't be so hard on yourself,' Guy ordered. He took a swig of wine. 'Did you tell Hamish how you felt?'

'No. We were married such a short time, and it was so. . .eventful, that I never got around to deciding what I wanted to say, let alone saying it. Three months after the wedding my father had a coronary,' Roxanne told him. 'I was struggling to come to terms with that when we

moved house—and I began to suspect Hamish
wasn't being honest about his finances—then I
discovered I was pregnant, and—and not much
later,' she said chokily, 'the police were knocking on the door to tell me I was a widow.'

Guy winced. 'You said that last few years
hadn't been easy, but you've taken one hell of a
thrashing,' he murmured.

As he moved across the sofa and put his arm
around her, she trembled. She had been on the
brink of crying so often as she talked, and now
his sympathy was too much. All of a sudden
tears were flooding from her eyes, rolling down
her cheeks, dripping off the end of her chin.

'I imagined life had improved, but the
traumas went on and on. It was horrible. Well,
being pregnant wasn't horrible,' Roxanne
gasped between sobs, 'except that I wasn't sure
about having a baby when I wasn't sure about—
about. . .' Guy had produced a box of tissues
and she scrubbed valiantly at her cheeks.
'Hamish being much older had put a distance
between me and my girlfriends, and everyone
else seemed to think I'd married him for his
money, so there wasn't anyone I could talk to. I
just pretended everything was great.' Roxanne
sniffed. 'But today I have talked, and it's been—
oh, Guy, thank you.'

Ruefully, he eyed her tear-stained face. 'I
always try to give a girl a good time.'

'And you have!'

She had meant to laugh, but still she cried. So much anguish and pain had been bottled up for so long, and now it poured out of her. Roxanne used a dozen paper handkerchiefs before she managed to calm down.

'Feeling better?' Guy asked as she blew her nose.

She grinned, sniffed, and reached for her wine. 'Much.'

'Why did Hamish decide to become an impresario?' he enquired when she had taken a few steadying sips.

'For the glitz and the glamour.'

'Gee whizz!'

Roxanne smiled. 'Maybe it leaves you cold, but he couldn't get enough. Sometimes he was co-producer on shows, and although it was an honorary post he got a great buzz from being connected with "the business",' she quoted archly, remembering how often the term had been bandied around, 'and from being able to name-drop when he met someone like, say, Athol. Athol thought Hamish walked on water, likewise a good number of other people, but, although he did have genuine friends, often people's liking for him had much to do with his generosity. And that had *everything* to do with Hamish's image of himself as the benevolent entrepreneur.' She sighed. 'His hand-outs were a way of building prestige and profile. He didn't want favours in return, he simply enjoyed people thanking him—and everyone else knowing.'

'His generosity was an ego trip?'

Roxanne nodded. 'I know he was generous to me, but——'

'Generous to you?' Guy demanded. 'He was generous at your expense! OK, he didn't know he was going to die, but he did know the money was running out—had run out—and yet he continued to finance shows and splash cash around his so-called friends and to hell with the consequences. He didn't give a damn about your security or that you'd suffered a battering before, all he cared about was his free-spending image of himself—the selfish, self-centred, irresponsible bastard!'

She stared, taken aback by the ferocity of his attack.

'He—he did help my father,' she stammered. 'When Dad died he'd regained his self-respect—courtesy of Hamish.'

'And you're everlastingly grateful?' Guy said tersely. 'Show me how he used to rake back his hair. What did he do—a hand straight in from his brow?'

The conversation veered, her confessional was over, and the remainder of the evening was spent on demonstrations and hearing more about the play. Talking about her past had not been easy, yet when she went to bed Roxanne felt cleansed, strengthened and, after two long years, strangely tranquil.

Roxanne was on all fours measuring the study floor when Guy arrived home on Monday evening. Concentrating on getting the dimensions right and with the radio playing an up-beat big-band number, the first she knew of his arrival was a thwack on her backside.

'Watch it!' she protested, only to find herself hauled into his arms and danced around the room in time to the music. 'Do I assume that Jonas/Hamish works?' she asked, laughing as he quickstepped her behind the desk and out again.

'You do. I needed something to hang him on, and you gave it to me.'

'The raking back of the hair?'

'And the specs. Mind you, the old villain's not all there yet, but he will be. He will be. Hi, Barney,' her partner grinned when the little boy scampered in from the garden to check out the hilarity. 'Want to dance?'

The twosome became a threesome, Barnaby clinging on to Guy's neck and giggling as they circled around.

'You do realise this 'orrible child walked in straight from the sandpit and now we're all covered in sand?' Roxanne enquired as the music came to an end.

'So what?' Guy dabbed a finger on the end of

the toddler's nose. 'We can fling off our clothes and go into the shower, can't we?'

'Yes!' shouted Barnaby.

The tiger eyes met Roxanne's. 'You, me and Mummy?' he murmured.

'Yes!' her son yelled.

Maybe it was due to being spun round, or maybe not, but all of a sudden her knees felt wobbly. 'I—I don't think so,' she said.

Guy grinned. 'You're right. I'd much rather it was just the two of us.'

'You and Barney?' she enquired, attempting to recover.

He affected enormous innocence. 'Who else?'

Guy's good humour lasted through dinner, through a blitz on the garden—clearing weeds and hacking down the grass should have been a chore, but it wasn't, not with him working beside her—through the subsequent unwinding session. But as they drank cups of bedtime coffee, his exhilaration faded and he became pensive. Was he having second thoughts about Jonas/Hamish? Roxanne wondered. Might the character not be as attainable as he had believed? Had he jumped at her suggestion too quickly and was now regretting it? She was on the point of asking, when Guy rose to his feet.

'I'm bushed,' he said, 'and I'm sure you must be, too.'

Roxanne was tired, but when she got to bed she could not sleep. Downstairs her grandfather clock chimed midnight, and later one o'clock, yet still she lay awake, haunted by a picture of her and Guy in the shower. His hair sleeked by the spray and his golden skin sluiced, he was smiling down at her. Hands bubbly with foam, he began to soap her breasts, dragging at her nipples, sliding his fingers down her stomach to caress the tender skin between her thighs, kissing her from time to time. And as she became aroused—arching her spine as the shock-waves of pleasure broke over her—so did he.

The creak of a floorboard outside on the landing broke into her thoughts. Roxanne sat up, listened, then threw back the sheet. Yesterday morning Barnaby had scaled the bars of his cot and padded along to find her. Could he have climbed out of his cot now? But it was dark and he would be sleepy, and instead of her room he might take a wrong turning. Her head filled with visions of him tumbling head over heels down the stairs, she flew across the room and flung open the door—but there was no sign of the little boy.

'Something the matter?' a voice asked, startling her, and she turned to see Guy sitting on the window-seat at the far end of the landing. Tousle-headed and barefoot, he wore a pair of boxer-shorts.

'I thought I heard Barnaby, but it must have been you.' Roxanne padded towards him. 'Can't you sleep?'

'No,' he said curtly.

'Why not? Are you thinking about the play?'

'The play?' He gave a strangled laugh. 'Hell, no.'

'Then what?'

Guy hesitated. 'If you must know, what I'm thinking about—what's been plaguing me ever since I said it—is you and me in the shower together.'

'Oh!'

His eyes narrowed. 'You've been thinking about it, too?'

'Um. Well,' Roxanne blustered, giving thanks for the darkness which hid her blushes. She tossed her head. 'Of course not!'

'You lying hound!'

With grand disdain, she ignored him. 'Goodnight,' she said, and, performing a swift one-hundred-and-eighty-degree turn, she marched off towards her room.

Guy caught her in the doorway. 'Goodnight be damned! Did you honestly believe that if we lived together we weren't going to end up sleeping together? And not just sleeping together, loving each other?' He cupped large hands over her shoulders. 'Rox, I love you,' he said, his voice low and serious. 'And I think you love me, too. You might not *want* to, but you do.'

'Guy, look——' she began.

He placed silencing fingers over her mouth.

'Shh. The only thing I want to look at tonight is you. All of you.' Catching hold of the narrow straps of her nightgown, he drew them from her shoulders and slowly, slowly, the silk slid down her body to rustle into a soft heap on the floor. 'You're beautiful,' he murmured, and as she gazed into his face she saw his excitement at seeing her naked. Now the golden flecks in his eyes were molten.

Reverently his hands moved over her body, stroking the full curve of her breasts, outlining the narrowness of her waist, sliding over her stomach to caress the dark, furry mound at her thighs.

'Oh, Guy,' she said, on a sob.

He was right, she did love him. All these weeks when she had been playing his games, when she had watched him playing with Barnaby, when he had made her laugh and comforted her, it had been building, until now she knew. She *knew*. But loving him would make everything so complicated. All her instincts insisted that she move away, but, beneath the melting gaze of his eyes and the seductive caresses of his hands, she was powerless. He drew her close, kissing her brow, her nose, her mouth, and then, suddenly, his arms wound tighter and he swung her up off her feet and carried her to the bed.

'I've waited so long for this,' Guy murmured, and started to kiss her again.

His mouth was hard and hot and persuasive. Roxanne wound her arms around his neck, rubbing her breasts against his chest and gasping as the mat of bronze hair scraped against the sensitive, swelling tips.

Guy withdrew a little, holding her away as his eyes toured her body. 'You have beautiful breasts,' he said, trickling long fingers over the taut curves, 'so round and firm and pointy. I want to taste them.'

As he bent his head to suckle at her nipples, her body arched in response and her head felt as though it had been split by lightning. Roxanne began to move her hands over him, stroking his shoulders, his back, his torso, absorbing the hot, moist feel of his skin through her palms and fingertips.

'I never noticed you stripping off,' she whispered as her hand followed the downward arrowing of tawny body hair across the flat plane of his stomach.

'You never noticed Superman?'

'Is that what it is?'

He smiled against her mouth. 'Did you notice how I've been sick with love for you these past few weeks?' he asked.

'Well. . .yes.'

'But you've never admitted it?'

'Well. . .no.'

Guy pulled her close again, a muscled thigh encroaching between hers, and as she felt the throb and thrust of his body an intense hunger filled her. Slowly at first, savouring the erotic sensation of naked skin on naked skin, but then more urgently, she moved her hips against him. He groaned, and his hands returned to her breasts, caressing, stroking, pinching at the swollen peaks. An explosion burst deep inside her, and another, and another.

As she cried out his name, he drove into her. Roxanne writhed beneath him, her fingernails digging into the firm flesh of his back, liquid fire rampaging through her veins. It had never been like this before, she thought dimly. She had never been lost in such swirling, velvety desire, never known this frenzy of need. But, all of a sudden, his driving rhythm stopped. Gasping in a breath, Guy waited for a long, charged moment, holding himself above her with every muscle tense and strained.

Roxanne looked deep into his eyes. She knew what he wanted to hear. She knew what she wanted to say.

'I love you,' she murmured, and his body covered hers and he took her.

'Will you marry me?' Guy asked, deep in the night. He stroked her cheek and smiled. 'Please.'

After making love for hours, Roxanne had been relaxed and dreamily drowsy, but now she came awake.

'I thought you didn't mind living in sin?' she queried.

'I don't, not for——'

'Have you lived in sin before?'

He shifted restlessly. 'A couple of times.'

'I haven't, and I'd like to try it.' Pushing herself up on to one elbow, she bent over and kissed his mouth. 'I'd like to be your mistress. It sounds deliciously wicked.'

'Your hair's wicked,' Guy muttered. 'When you brush it across my chest like that it brings me to a state of such highly concentrated pleasure that——' he groaned as she swayed, tantalisingly drawing the long tresses over his skin '—— it's amazing I haven't ended up in intensive care.'

Roxanne laughed. 'Want to risk it again?'

'Just once.' He sighed. 'Or maybe twice, or. . .'

CHAPTER EIGHT

Two days later Guy again asked her to marry him, and a couple of days after that. Each time, Roxanne made a light-hearted quip and escaped into evasion—and each time guilt had consumed her. He deserved a straight answer to a straight question, and the answer she longed to give was yes. But. . .

No matter how much she loved him, if she were to marry him she would be boarding that roller-coaster again. Yet should she? Could she? Worldly fortunes were not an issue—a modest living would suit her fine—what lay at stake was her peace of mind. But there was nothing peaceful in being blindly pitched from heights into unpredictable depths or vice versa, in never knowing what lurked behind the next corner, in being continually taken by surprise—and wasn't that what a future with Guy held? He had spoken of his career failing, Roxanne thought disconsolately. Maybe it would not happen this year, or next, or ever, yet the risk would always be there. And if he shot to stardom as everyone predicted then that, too, could be erratic. Some might thrive on perpetual uncertainty, but not her—not now. What she wanted was a life immune from chop and change; structured, stable and reliable.

Roxanne gave a soundless scream. Unfortunately, she also wanted *him*—to love and to cherish, for ever and ever. Amen. So, should she forget her misgivings, ignore her fears? In the bliss of his embrace, it would be easy to do. Yet she hesitated. Having made one ill-conceived and blinkered rush into marriage, she was determined to get it right this time—for her sake, for his, for Barnaby's. She must not be either an ostrich or an optimist.

'Remember I told you how the pew had been salvaged from scrap?' Roxanne asked, a few nights later.

As soon as Barnaby had been put to bed, the magnet of desire had drawn them together, relentlessly kissing, touching, undressing, and they had made love, and again two hours after that. Now they were lying on the sofa, lazily talking and half watching the late film.

'Mmm,' Guy said drowsily.

'I met the foreman of the demolition team this morning and he told me they were knocking down an old hotel, so I went along. I've found a stained-glass window of a flower garden in pinks, blues and greens which he says is going for the price of a beer. It'd add a wonderful oomph to your study. What do you think?'

Idly he teased strands of her hair through his fingers. 'Sounds too good to miss—and so are you. Sweetheart, when are we going to get married?'

Roxanne quaked, hearing the question ring out like the peal of an ominous bell.

'Don't rush me,' she demurred.

'I'm not, I'm willing to live in sin for a while if that's what makes you happy.' His arm tightened around her. 'However, don't imagine I'll settle for us living together indefinitely, because it's not going to happen. I'm the old-fashioned type who believes in old-fashioned matrimony.'

'Yessir!'

'Rox, if the media gets to hear of you—us— they're going to start poking around and asking questions,' Guy continued, ignoring her flippancy, 'and I don't want your name splashed over the tabloids as my live-in lover. Sure, the idea's neither shocking or new, but we're talking about you and me here, not the rest of the world, and between us I want everything to be. . .proper.'

'But it's less than a week since—since we realised how we felt about each other,' Roxanne protested, 'so the Press aren't likely to find us out, not for a long time.'

'We hope,' he said darkly. 'And as for realising how we feel, it's four years since I fell in love with you. Honest,' he grinned when she lifted her head from his shoulder to stare. 'I'd always ridiculed the idea of love at first sight, but then I saw you on the set of *Assignment Paris* and——' he clasped a hand to his heart '—where my world had been monochrome, you changed it to glorious Technicolor.'

Roxanne arched a brow. 'And which script did you steal that line from?' she enquired.

'I made it up myself. Playwrights aren't that corny.'

'Are you sure it wasn't lust at first sight?' she said, laughing.

'There could have been some lust involved,' Guy agreed, and made a wild bite at her neck. 'Certainly when we went into a clinch you had a fantastic effect on my erogenous zones, but it was much more than physical. I didn't understand why, I couldn't explain it to myself, but suddenly I knew you were "the one". OK, OK, I know it sounds like I'm being corny again, but it's what happened. Why did you think I felt so cut up about being ignored?' he demanded. 'There I was damn near standing on my head to make an impression and you barely acknowledged my existence. Up to that point I'd not had too much bother attracting the opposite sex——'

'I wouldn't have thought you'd have had *any* bother,' she interrupted.

'Maybe,' he said enigmatically. 'The crew thought my traipsing around like a love-sick loon was the joke of the year, while Prue. . .' His mouth twisted into the mockery of a smile.

'She swore your coolness was a deliberate come-on.'

'Prue knew how you felt?'

'That you'd knocked me out? Yes. I had to explain to her why our relationship must end.'

'And you ended it because of *me*?' Roxanne enquired, her grey eyes at their widest.

'It was the honest thing to do. I couldn't string her along,' Guy protested. 'At the time I was determined that even if you did have another lover, which was what I assumed, I would——'

She poked him in the ribs. 'Did it never occur to you that I might simply not like the magnificent Mr Slaney?'

'No.' He squirmed away. 'And the magnificent Mr Slaney wasn't being swollen-headed, he just knew that he'd never registered.'

'Why didn't you drop a few hints about how you felt?'

'Would it have made any difference?'

'At that time?' Roxanne thought back. 'I doubt it.'

'So do I. Your father's troubles used too much emotional energy to leave any spare for a romance. But I didn't drop hints because, one, strong-arming isn't my style, and, two, I hoped I'd grow on you. Telling Prue I wanted out caused one hell of a row,' he reflected. 'Our relationship had been casual, I'd never sworn undying devotion or anything like that, yet she was very resentful, very aggressive. At the time she couldn't decide whom she disliked the most, me or you,' Guy said ruefully. 'And when you got married she had a field day with the sarcasm and cutting remarks.'

'She wasn't pleased when she first found me here on the night of the party. Then I didn't understand why, but now. . .'

'Now you do,' he completed as her voice trailed away. 'And now you understand why the idea of a link-up between you and the Arabian dreamboat didn't thrill me, either. I did my best to make a joke of it, but when I stepped into your hall and saw that crumpled bed, something inside me snapped.'

She cast him a quizzical look. 'You can't have been in love with me for the entire past four years?'

'No, by the time *Assignment Paris* was wrapped up I'd accepted we were a lost cause, and after a month or two I decided I'd recovered.'

'Then you forgot about me?'

Guy pursed his lips. 'No-o. Every time I saw Hamish's name in the papers I thought of you afresh. But then you arrived at my door and——'

'Glorious Technicolor?'

He shook his head. 'I was seeing things from a different perspective by then.'

'You weren't too sure about my marriage?' Roxanne suggested.

'It had altered things,' he agreed slowly. 'Even so, to meet you again when you were a widow and find you had a lover seemed a peculiarly vicious kick from fate. That's when I realised that, like it or not, I'd never properly got over you.'

Roxanne thought about what he had said. 'You must have had. . .girlfriends over the past four years?' she questioned.

His mouth curved. 'I haven't been celibate, if that's what you're getting at. But neither have I lived with another woman, and I don't want to——' Guy made quotation marks in the air '—"live" with you. I know plenty of couples who do, and good luck to them, but to my mind it's a second-rate arrangement for those who aren't entirely committed. Rox, you and I have everything going for us,' he said, his voice picking up an urgency. 'We like each other as people, we love each other, the sex is bloody fantastic— yes?'

'Yes,' she had to agree.

'Plus Barney and I get on well together.'

'Barney thinks you're the sun, moon and stars gift-wrapped.'

'So why don't we fix a date for, say some time before Christmas? It's no great headache,' he protested, when she frowned.

Roxanne begged to differ. For days, the marriage dilemma had been making her head throb, and so did Guy's determination. Why must he push? Why couldn't he let things rest—for a while, at least? The love they shared was too new and too precious to be disrupted and yet, if she confessed that *she* was not entirely committed—that she harboured doubts which were still being thought through—disrupted it must be. . .or ended? Dismay chilled her skin. She could not bear to risk losing Guy, not yet. She needed to draw this happiness around her like a comforting quilt, needed to bathe in their mutual delight. Roxanne sighed silently. As he had been honest with Prue, she knew she must be honest with him—and she would be. Soon.

'Salim had had a headache,' she announced, as if making an off-the-cuff comment and not a deliberate diversion. 'You remember he spoke of relief? He was referring to two aspirin.'

For a moment Guy surveyed her in silence, then obligingly he grinned. 'You reckon I should take a couple of aspirin now?'

'Now? You mean——'

Taking hold of her hand, he brought it to his thigh. 'That's what I mean,' he said huskily.

The diversion had worked.

Roxanne had been watching and waiting for the taxi, and as it drew up outside she rushed to open the door.

'Success?' she grinned as Guy staggered into the hall carrying the stained-glass panel.

'Success. Removing it took time, but it's in

perfect condition. You're right,' he said as they gazed in admiration, 'it'll give the study a touch of magic.' Propping his booty against the wall, he drew her close and kissed her. 'I don't suppose you'd care to add more magic to my life?' he enquired.

Roxanne wound her arms around his neck. Barnaby was in bed, the chicken casserole she had made for dinner could keep, and—yes, please, yes—she wanted more of his searching kisses, more soaring desire, more of the burn, the heat, the rapture.

'What did you have in mind?' she asked, smiling.

'I'd like you to agree to marry me.'

Her smile evaporated. For over a week Guy had made no further reference to the future, and she had hoped he had settled for living in the present. Now she recognised it as a vain hope— and she also knew that evasion was not only dishonest, but unfair. He was not stupid, he had to be aware she was stringing him along, and she owed him something better. Much better. Roxanne swallowed. She must spell out her doubts and fears, what was good for her, what she required from life. It might clash with what she needed right now—and with what he was able to give—but still she must speak. Yet when she opened her mouth, the sentences cleaved to her throat.

'You know what the trouble is?' Guy

demanded. 'There's a part of you which still belongs to Hamish.' He broke from her, savagely thrusting his hands into the pockets of his jeans. 'The pair of you might have been hopelessly mismatched, and your marriage might have been destined to fail, but as I never really got over you, so you haven't got over him.'

Roxanne stared, knocked askew by the unexpected accusation. 'That's not true!' she protested. 'I told you I didn't love him.'

'There are many different kinds of love, a multitude of hang-ups,' he snarled, 'and for some reason you appear to believe you'd be compromising your relationship with damned Hamish if you join forces with me.'

'I don't!'

'You deny that whenever I talk about marriage you fill the moat and pull up the drawbridge?'

'No, but——'

'I thought it was odd when you were so adamant about no one knowing that Hamish had lost his money, and if you'd got him out of your system it wouldn't matter, you'd be willing for him to be seen as he was, warts and all,' Guy pronounced, in a steel-tipped voice. 'Instead, you're doing your utmost to protect him.'

'I'm not protecting Hamish,' she objected.

'Like hell! You want the world to believe he was the all-conquering hero, the ultimate success, the caring husband, and never mind that he built up a mountain of debts and left you to deal with them.' A nerve jumped in his temple. 'I hoped you and I had a future, I *believed* we had, but every time I take one step towards it I fall headlong over a tripwire—Hamish!'

'You're wrong,' Roxanne insisted.

'Then you'll marry me?' he came back at her.

Her insides clenched. 'Guy, I—we need to talk about that.'

'Talk?' His laugh was bleak. 'If you can't give me a straight "yes", forget it.'

'But——'

'You reckon it'll take a month to find alternative accommodation—that's OK,' he steamrollered on. 'But as soon as you're ready to leave, do.'

He was refusing to talk? He wanted her gone? She had anticipated problems, but she had not reckoned on his ending their love-affair right now. Roxanne gazed at him, stunned by the enormity of what he was saying and of what she was losing. Guy would not come to her bed tonight. He would not hold her close. He would never again tell her he loved her.

'You're—you're going out?' she floundered as he strode towards the door.

'I'm going to get drunk,' he retorted, 'so don't bother waiting up. And I could be working late over the next week, so don't wait up then, either.'

She cast him a wary look. 'I thought rehearsals were going well?'

'They are, but the nearer we get to first night, the more dedicated the director becomes. Damn,' he muttered as he opened the door.

'What's the matter?'

Guy scowled. 'I told Emma I'd call in tomorrow evening,' he said, and shrugged. 'Oh, well, when I don't turn up she'll have yet another reason to slander me.'

'I'll go,' Roxanne said quickly. She had often wondered what the old lady was like—surely she couldn't be as cantankerous as he claimed?—and even listening to grumbles would be preferable to sitting alone for what threatened to be night after night after night. 'Barney can have an afternoon nap and I'll take him along,' she said when Guy hesitated.

'Good idea,' he said. 'Goodnight.'

A moment later, the door slammed shut behind him.

For the first quarter of an hour, visiting Emma did seem like a good idea. A thin-faced, cold-eyed woman of haughty bearing, she might have allowed Roxanne only a suspicious glance and a cursory greeting, but her pleasure on seeing Barnaby was genuine. His presence ensured everything swung smoothly along—until the matron appeared with news of a bed-ridden inmate who had heard the little boy had arrived and please could she take a peek? A battle ensued, Emma peevishly insisting that

Barnaby was *her* visitor so he must stay her with her, and the endlessly smiling matron vowing he would only be gone for a minute.

'Do you mind if I take him?' the matron appealed to Roxanne at last, placing her in the position of adjudicator and putting her on the spot, and she had felt unable to object.

Left alone with Emma, she gamely tried to make conversation, but whatever she said, whether it was congratulations on her full recovery from the stroke, or praise for the long spell of fine weather, or a comment on her comfortably furnished room, the old lady chose not to agree. Piqued at being overruled, and holding Roxanne responsible, she was argumentative, contrary and, at times, downright objectionable. In describing her as 'sour' Guy had been generous, Roxanne decided as the promised minute stretched to a hard-going ten. In her opinion, the 'old bird' was undiluted sulphuric acid.

'Another ten days and Guy opens in his new play,' Roxanne remarked jauntily.

'Speak up,' came the instruction.

'Guy will soon be appearing in the West End,' she said, louder.

Although Emma's hearing had been acute when Barnaby had been around, now she demanded that every other sentence be repeated. Either the batteries in her hearing-aid had abruptly expired—or this was yet another example of her perversity.

'Humph!' Censorious hands were folded. 'Acting is trivial.'

'No, it's not.'

'Speak up.'

Roxanne gritted her teeth. After being friendly and pleasant and trying to jolly the old lady along, her patience was wearing thin—and she was damned if she'd allow every word she uttered to be shot down in flames.

'A good play or film gives a great deal of enjoyment to a great many people,' she insisted. 'They provide an escape from the everyday world, a refreshing break and stimulation for the mind. Culture in all its forms is a vital part of the human experience. Actors and acting enrich our lives. Guy——'

Emma sniffed. 'Pity he can't find something better to do than lounging around.'

'Guy does not lounge around! He works hard and seriously. He puts tremendous energy into his acting.'

'Wasted energy. He should be using it for something worth while.'

'Like what?' Roxanne demanded. 'I suppose you'd rather he was——' she searched around for an occupation and said the first which came into her head '—a bank clerk?'

'Much!' Emma snapped.

'But why? Being a bank clerk is no better and no worse than being an actor, it's just different.'

'Different in that a bank clerk brings home a

pay-cheque at the end of the month, each month, and has guaranteed employment. Don't hear of too many banks closing down, do you?' her companion said slyly, and sniffed again. 'Acting is a job for fools.'

Roxanne glared. Over the years Guy had given up hundreds of hours on this woman's behalf, and what did he get in return—not one word of thanks, no allegiance, not the least fidelity.

'Guy is a level-headed, caring, *practising* human being!' she said heatedly. 'He's also very good at what he does. But if he did find himself out of work, do you think he'd just stand around? No way. In a very short time he'd find something else to do, and he'd made a success of it!'

'Speak up.'

She clenched her fists. 'Guy is associated with real life, with the real world,' she announced in piercing tones, 'which means that, as much as he enjoys acting, he would never do it *in extremis*. Guy does not fit into the "gambler" category!'

'There's no need to shout. I take it you and he are. . .' she received a withering look '. . .friends?'

'Close friends,' Roxanne declared. 'Extremely close.'

The thin-lipped mouth turned down. 'I thought you'd have had more sense than to throw in your lot with someone like him. After all, you do have Barnaby to consider.'

'Guy is the best thing that ever happened to Barney, and he's the best thing that ever happened to *me*! I'd consider it a privilege to throw in my lot with him. Indeed, I'd accompany him to the ends of the earth,' Roxanne vowed, then stopped short, listening to what she was saying and what she had said. 'What did your husband do for a living?' she asked, suddenly wanting to smile, sing, turn cartwheels.

'He was a lecturer.'

'So he had a regular salary and secure employment?'

'And an irritating habit of laughing at his own jokes and dropping cigar ash all over the place,' Emma denounced, and sped on to spitefully assassinate yet another character.

When Guy arrived home that night, Roxanne contrived to be in the bathroom. It was late, though not too late, yet, although she was determined they must talk, she had been wary of waiting for him in the living-room. If he found her sitting there he could sense that she wanted a discussion—and avoid it. So to have just stepped under the shower seemed appropriately *casual*.

'Hi,' she called, hearing him reach the top of the stairs. 'How were the rehearsals?'

'Fine.' For a moment he hesitated, then he

came and stood outside the door. 'How did you get on with Emma?' he asked.

'Wonderfully. She was ill-tempered, impolite and malicious—and she devoted a good quarter of an hour bad-mouthing you.'

'That was wonderful?'

'Sorry?' Roxanne shouted, over the spray.

Where the old lady's feigning of deafness had been petulance, hers was a ploy. One which worked to perfection—for Guy came into the bathroom and spoke to her through the opaque glass of the shower cubicle.

'You enjoyed Emma doing a hatchet job on me?' he enquired drily.

'I didn't enjoy it, but I'm glad she did, because in putting her straight about you I learned something myself. I learned that——' Roxanne slid open the door and smiled out at him. 'Ask me to marry you again,' she said.

He frowned at her dripping figure. 'No.'

'What do you mean, no?' she protested.

'I mean that defending me seems to have brought about a change of heart, and that's fine.' An air of weary aggravation crossed his face. 'But it doesn't eliminate the Hamish factor.' He turned. 'Goodnight.'

She stared at him in dismay. So much for being *casually* in the shower, so much for thinking that once she mentioned marriage he would be bound to listen. She would have done better to have accosted him in the living-room, with chains and handcuffs close at hand!

'Guy, you can't just go,' she implored.

He flung a look back over his shoulder. 'Try and stop me.'

Roxanne did. She leapt out, lunged, grabbed his arms from behind and, with a superhuman tug, heaved him backwards with her into the cubicle.

'Hey!' he protested, taken by surprise. Stumbling over the step, he struggled to keep his balance. 'What the hell do you think you're doing?'

The jet streamed down like monsoon rain, wetting his head, splashing his shoulders, making dark stains on his jeans.

'I want us to talk, and you wanted us to take a shower together,' she panted, arms locked around his waist and speaking into his shoulder-blades, 'so we're going to do both.'

'I never wanted to take a shower in my damn *clothes*!' Guy wrenched around to face her. 'Look at me,' he raged, swiping a hank of sodden hair out of his eyes. 'Just look what you've done!'

His shirt was a damp rag, his sneakers squelched, a droplet of water fell off the end of his nose.

Roxanne put her hand over her mouth. 'Oh, dear.'

'Don't you dare snigger!' he threatened.

'About the Hamish factor, there isn't one,' she

gabbled. 'There never has been. You thought he was getting in the way, but he wasn't. It was you—or rather, it was your job. You see——'

'What d'you think you're doing now?' Guy demanded as her fingers went to the buttons on his shirt.

'I'm going to undress you and take liberties with your person, and——' she gulped in a breath, '—then you'll be forced to ask me to marry you.'

'You reckon?'

Roxanne said a silent prayer. 'I reckon.'

'You're giving me the hard option?'

'I am.'

'You could always propose to me,' Guy remarked as she peeled the waterlogged cotton from his shoulders.

Her spirits lifted. All of a sudden, Roxanne knew everything was going to be fine, wonderful, ecstasy.

'I prefer to be conventional,' she told him.

'Hauling a man kicking and screaming into a shower and stripping him is conventional?'

'I thought you were remarkably docile.'

'I didn't want to wake Barney.'

Roxanne smiled. 'How considerate.'

Soon his clothes had been dumped in the washbasin and Guy was naked.

'Want to take those liberties,' he murmured as clouds of steam rose around them, 'or are you desperate to talk first?'

Her pulses raced. Imagining them in the shower and *being* here with him were two different things. The thrum of the water, the trickle of it over her skin, the glossed look of his, added an erotic dimension she had never anticipated. Guy had not even touched her, yet her legs were weak, she trembled, she ached for him so much that it hurt.

'Talking could wait,' Roxanne said breathily.

He smiled and, as in her dream, he rubbed a tablet of fragrant-smelling soap between his palms, then, when a foamy lather had been created, he raised his hands to her breasts. Her heart began to pump. His touch slow and sure, Guy soaped the rounded undersides, weighing her breasts in his hands, then his fingers moved upwards. As he caressed the tight peaks, her spine straightened and she stood there with eyes closed, a slender, water-glossed statue submitting to the exquisite torture.

'Lift up your hair,' he instructed, and when she had raised the sleek, dripping curtain he washed her shoulders and down her back.

More foam, more caresses, and his hands slithered around her thighs to seek out the petalled nerve-centre of her being which he stroked and fondled until she cried out aloud. Guy kissed her, holding her close until the tremors of her body had ceased.

'Now your turn,' he murmured.

Roxanne looked at him wide-eyed. 'My turn?'

'You didn't imagine this?' he asked, and when she shook her head he smiled, and handed her the soap.

If being lathered was a sensual joy, so lathering possessed its own excitement. As she soaped the hard planes of his body, her fingers shook and her heart beat out of tune. When she had touched him before he had been dry, but now his skin was slippery wet and seemed charged with a thousand volts.

'The readers of *Movie Chat* magazine are people of some discernment,' Roxanne breathed, reaching his backside.

Guy grinned. 'You think?'

'I know.'

He laughed, and scooped up some of her bubbles. Now there was mutual lathering. Dizzily sliding, gliding, slithering fingers. Her breathing quickened. And his.

'Bed,' he muttered.

He was kissing her, urgently and desperately, his body heavy on hers. The sheets were cool. His skin was hot and damp. A frenzy built, and need—a demanding need, an aching need, an overwhelming need.

'Hell,' Guy groaned, 'do you think I'll ever manage to make love to you calmly and coolly all the way through?'

Roxanne put her hand on his hip. 'I hope not.'

With a muttered cry, he entered her, and she felt him in the deepest places of her womb. She moved beneath him and suddenly the world was shooting away, and she was falling, spinning, clutching, bursting, rising. . .rising. . . rising.

It was long after midnight before Roxanne got around to explaining why she had hesitated to accept his proposal.

'I was terrified of the unpredictable, of ups and downs, but I was viewing life with you in terms of life with my father and Hamish,' she said, 'and I was wrong. You don't follow compulsions.'

'No?' Guy ran his fingers along her thigh. 'I wouldn't be too sure about that.'

Roxanne kissed him. 'You don't follow any other compulsions,' she amended. 'You don't allow circumstances to run away with you, you do your best to control them. So if there are ups and downs, they'll be ones I can cope with.'

'Ones *we* can cope with,' he told her.

'Yes.' She smiled. 'That was another mistake I made. I was imagining being hit by the unexpected, but whatever happens it won't be unexpected, because you'll tell me, you'll share. One of the worst things about the past was that neither Dad nor Hamish shared,' she said soberly. 'They simply left me to find out on my own, and then it was such a shock and I felt so deceived. And so frustrated, because maybe I could have helped.'

'Like you helped me with Jonas,' Guy smiled.

'Our helping has been mutual,' Roxanne said, and kissed him. 'When I started to tell you about Hamish,' she continued, 'I seriously wondered if it was going to end up as a tirade. You see, although I have mixed feelings about him, I also think he was a selfish bastard.'

'You do?'

'When he died and I discovered all those debts—thoughtless debts, often unnecessary debts—I *hated* him! He'd stopped me working, he'd made me dependent, he'd wanted a child, yet all the time he knew there was no hope of supporting me or a baby.'

Guy pulled the sheet closer around them. 'He should have made some kind of provision. He should have saved *something*.'

Roxanne sighed agreement. 'So there I was resenting him like crazy, while everyone else was sending letters of sympathy extolling this marvellous man! I knew being bitter wasn't going to get me anywhere, and I did my best to pull down the shutters and forget Hamish and the past, but I wasn't very successful.' She gave a wry smile. 'The surprising thing is that somewhere along the way I seem to have become fatalistic.'

'You don't hate him any more?'

'No. OK, he ransacked my life, but he's gone. And even though I regret our marriage, I've never regretted having Barney.'

Guy looked at her through the dim light. 'It's because of Barney that you've concealed the truth about Hamish, isn't it? And why you want it to remain a secret?' She nodded. 'You'd rather he didn't know his father was. . .a reprobate?'

'That, and——' Roxanne sighed again. 'The way I see it, if the public perception of Hamish remains constant, then when Barney grows up he won't be of any interest to the media. And should something bring him to their attention, he'll simply be tagged as the impresario's son. However, if at any time it's discovered that Hamish wasn't the virtuoso he always claimed to be, then certain members of the Press are going to sit up and take notice.' She grimaced. 'I told you how he was economical with the truth—well, a couple of reporters sensed that he could be hoodwinking them and were not pleased. They never managed to unearth anything, but——'

'If the facts came out you think they'd seek revenge by publicising them?' Guy suggested.

'It's possible, though, revenge or not, Hamish Dunn's being revealed as a fraud makes a good story.' Roxanne shifted on the pillow. 'But the vital factor in all this is his death. Hamish was killed when he smashed his Mercedes into a motorway bridge. The accident happened in broad daylight, during sparse traffic, when he was in good health.'

Guy frowned, recalling the headlines. 'He fell asleep at the wheel?'

She nodded. 'He'd been chasing around the country trying to catch up with first a composer, then a lyricist, who were rumoured to have a musical in the offing, and in two days he'd driven a vast number of miles and taken very little rest.'

'He had thoughts of backing a show even then?' Guy protested.

'He was so deep in debt, why not go even deeper?' she said astringently. 'But the point is that, at the time, the police asked me if there was any possibility of his having committed suicide. They explained that it was something they had to raise, and they were satisfied with my answer, but——'

'What did you say?' he cut in.

'That Hamish had been walking on air ever since my pregnancy had been confirmed a month or so earlier, and I could produce hundreds of witnesses to prove it. He'd been going around telling everyone he met, from the postman to the street-cleaner,' she explained, 'and giving them huge cigars.'

Guy chuckled. 'I have to admit that, although he was a rat, he sounds to have been a charming one.'

'He was. And he'd never have taken his own life. He and Janet had been desperate for a family, but it hadn't happened, and now there was no way he'd have missed out on being a father—even if the bailiffs were poised to break down the door. His financial position must have worried him, but no way was he in despair. Hamish was the type who always believed something would turn up. But if his debts became public knowledge,' she continued, 'then the Press might re-examine his death and raise the possibility of suicide.'

'And Barney would be saddled with that for the rest of his life?'

Roxanne nodded. 'The media have long memories—scandals of the sixties are still being aired today, made into films even, and never mind the personal anguish involved. And although the fuss would pass over him now, should Barney come into the news at a later date the old stories would appear and the tongues would start wagging, and——' she shuddered '—it could affect him. My father's gambling had a traumatic effect on my brother,' she explained. 'Paul found the shame and embarrassment hard to handle the first time around, but when it started again he went wild. He'd warned that if Dad went back on his word and put us through all the misery again he'd disown him, and——' tears welled as she remembered the ugly scenes, the shouting, the pleading '—and as soon as he realised Dad was gambling again he took active steps to get as far away as possible.'

Guy's arm closed around her. 'That's why he went to Australia?'

She nodded. 'He flew out a week before Dad's court appearance. He refused to come back when I assured him that Dad had stopped gambling, and he wouldn't even return for his funeral.'

'Oh, sweetheart,' he murmured.

'What my father did blighted Paul's life——' her chin lifted '—but I don't intend to allow what his father did to blight Barney's.'

'It won't.' Guy held her tight. 'Rox, it won't. I promise.'

'Thanks.'

'And now,' he said, 'before we go to sleep there's just one more thing I want to know.'

'What's that?'

'Will you marry me?'

Roxanne's mouth spread into a wide grin. 'Yes, please.'

CHAPTER NINE

ROXANNE pulled another newspaper from the heap which crowded the bed and read selected phrases out loud. '"A milestone event in the history of the theatre. A towering performance. Guy Slaney's acting has a hard, compassionate luminosity. He blazes like a forest fire."'

Lying beside her, Guy yawned. 'There was no need to phone the newsagent and have him deliver every single paper printed in the land, we knew last night the play was a hit.'

'Just,' she said and grinned, thinking of the standing ovation he had received, the cheers, the pats on the back, the delirious joy of the cast, the fans who had congregated outside the theatre, the incessant pop of flashbulbs.

It had been a wonderful evening. She had felt so proud of him, and so pleased. And so happy to be introduced to everyone as the woman who would soon be his wife.

'"Guy Slaney is so understated off stage,"' Roxanne read, '"that when you see him on it you can't help but wonder where the power of transformation comes from———"' She broke off. 'I don't think you're understated,' she said indignantly.

'What do you think?'

'I think—I'll tell you later. "But all the best actors are born to dissimulate,"' she continued, refusing to be side-tracked, '"and last night Slaney proved he *is* one of the best. His portrayal of Jonas Willoughby is magnetic, riveting, sexy, and the way he lets us know the man is posturing, almost by osmosis, rates as sheer brilliance."' Another paper was leafed through, another column eagerly scanned. '"A potent production, one where, yet again, Guy Slaney displays the quality which has marked his film and television performances—you can't take your eyes off him." It's true,' she said. 'I couldn't.'

Guy nuzzled his lips against her shoulder. 'Ah, but you're biased.'

'A bit.'

'A bit?' he protested.

'A lot, and yet the strange thing is that although I knew I was watching you, and I knew the character bore a passing resemblance to Hamish, as the play progressed I forgot. You made me see Jonas, just Jonas. That's a remarkable achievement.'

'Aw, shucks.'

'It is,' she insisted. She rumpled his hair; he rebelled. There was some horseplay. It was a little while later before the next critique could be scrutinised.

'"When I saw Slaney's interpretation of

Hamlet six years ago, I realised I was in the company of a maestro,"' Roxanne quoted.

Guy groaned. 'There's more rubbish written about acting than has ever come down a builder's chute! All it would have needed was for me to have missed with Jonas, and *Assignment Paris* to have been televised straight afterwards, and that line would have read "when I saw Slaney in Hamlet I knew I was in the company of a nohoper."'

She frowned at him. 'The possible proximity of *Assignment Paris* to the play troubled you? That's what made you so anti?'

He nodded. 'This is a high-profile production, and if I'd flopped every director and casting department in the industry would have known. Add *zee gendarme* on top of it and——' Guy sliced a finger across his throat.

Roxanne dispensed with the papers. 'Instead of which you're a resounding success,' she grinned.

'For a few months, and that's all I need, because by then I'll be legally bound to a highly bankable interior decorator who'll be able to keep me in great style.'

'I thought that if all else failed you were going into furniture removal.'

'Nah, I'd rather be a rich woman's plaything. Especially if that rich woman happens to be exceedingly beautiful and have the most——'

Guy's hand moved beneath the sheet. '—delectable body in the whole of creation.' He raised a brow. 'Would you like me to blaze like a forest fire?'

'Again?'

'Being a success makes the adrenalin flow.'

The fire raged hot, passion seared, and when Barnaby charged in half an hour later they were lying together, dreamily replete.

'Perfect timing,' Guy remarked as the toddler scrambled on to the bed. 'It's not often you sleep late, buddy boy, but you do have a flair for choosing the right moment.'

'I'd say your sister let him stay up last night,' Roxanne said. She tickled her son's tummy. 'Yes?'

Barnaby grinned at her, and at Guy. 'Kiss,' he demanded, and kisses were received and given.

'Two months today,' Guy said, when the little boy had wriggled down between them, 'you and me and Mummy are going to dress up in our best clothes and go to church. And while you sit very, very quietly—with your Uncle Paul who's flying over from Australia, and a mammoth Slaney contingent comprising new grandparents, aunts, uncles and cousins—your mummy and I are going to promise to love each other.'

'Till death us do part,' Roxanne murmured as his hand found hers.

Guy smiled. 'And afterwards,' he continued,

'your mum and I are going to snatch a short honeymoon, and then we shall come home and live happily ever after.' He grinned down at the listening child. 'What do you think of that?'

As Barnaby considered the idea, his small nose wrinkled. 'Brrrrhhh,' he pronounced, and then he giggled.

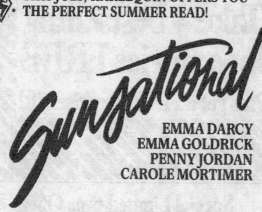